FINAL JOURNEY

A MARINE'S DESTINY

Frederick Bruce

ISBN 978-1-959182-02-3 (paperback)
ISBN 978-1-959182-03-0 (digital)

Lone Wildcat Books

(562) 437-3888

100 Oceangate F-12
Long Beach, CA 90802

Printed in the United States of America

Dedicated

To the men and women in the armed forces
who serve their country, never asking why,
but always stepping forward to do their job

Contents

Chapter One
Coming Home

He was coming home. Afghanistan was forever in his rear view mirror. To his grade school classmates and to his family, he was known as Terry Ward. The name that appears on his discharge papers is Terrence Joseph Ward. But to his close friends and Marine buddies, he was just known as TJ.

TJ's close friend was Ronald Charles Mason. They were together in high school, college and eventually in the service of the United States Marines Corps. By all accounts, the two men were inseparable. Their activities seemed to parallel each other. If you looked for, and found Ron Mason, you would also find TJ, and vice versa.

Unlike their previous years together, TJ was coming home alone. Ron came home several months earlier. Ron Mason had previously arrived in the United States with a contingent of assigned Marines. They had accompanied a casket carrying his remains. The scene was all too familiar for many who had observed the procedures for those who paid the ultimate price in service to their country. TJ felt that he had become a lost soul. Thoughts of his future were blurred. For all practical purposes, the future was nonexistent to him.

Although much of his previous memorable experiences included time spent with Ron Mason, TJ was consumed with the events that transpired on their final day together. On that day in Afghanistan, TJ and Ron were part of a group designated to proceed forward in an attempt to secure a village. When trying to adjust his ammunition belt, TJ found the strap to be faulty and his ammunition belt became unhinged. He was held back to adjust his equipment. In his place, Ron led the group and went forward in the duty assignment.

Within a matter of minutes, a bomb went off. In that instant, the life of Ron Mason ended. When news came back to the troops, TJ was stunned. His feelings were that life had also ended for him. It was not the first loss of life that he had experienced. He had been prepared and had previously experienced similar deadly events. But he was not able to cope with the loss of Ron Mason.

As he was coming home, he felt that he was just going through the motions. Before his discharge, the military psychologists and psychiatrists had spent time with TJ. Over time, it was their opinion that an intervention was needed. The prognosis they rendered was that TJ was going through a form of survivor's guilt. To TJ, this was a misdiagnosis. He understood survivor's guilt—thinking and feeling why did he survive, but his fellow Marine did not. No, this was not the same. Not just that he and Ron were close friends, but it was the manner in which the situation unfolded.

It could have been him. He's the one that most likely should have been coming home in a box. Because of the failure of the strap on his ammunition belt, Ron died instead of him. He could not adjust his head to that situation. It should have been him. Or maybe it could have, or should have, been both of them. While these thoughts circled in his head, TJ would drift in and out of sleep during the flight.

At times when he was awake, TJ's mind continued to wander as he tried to put his thoughts in place. How did he get to this point in his life? He started to think back to his childhood and the early years in his family.

TJ came from a very dysfunctional family. He didn't know it at the time. To him, as he was growing up, his family situation seemed normal. He knew no other comparison. There was constant turmoil in his family. Although both parents worked, they constantly moved. They were not able to financially exist in any one place.

TJ had adopted the feelings that his parents were constant victims. Whatever happened to them was never their fault—they were never responsible. At various times, his parents used their own parents and siblings to co-sign for the purchases of vehicles and to obtain various loans. When the payment obligations were not met, their co-signers were visited or contacted at home or at their place of employment regarding the unpaid obligations for which they had co-signed.

TJ, feeling great loyalty to his parents, continued to attribute the situation to bad luck or just being victims of bad circumstances that were beyond their control. Any knock at the door or ringing of the telephone caused anxiety for the children in the family. The first thought was that it was not going to be a friendly contact. Arguments ensued, but there never seemed to be a solution. The strained relations that TJ's parents had with their own parents and siblings also resulted in a loss of association for the children with their cousins.

The parents never communicated or discussed anything with the children, even though the events would have an ultimate impact on them. The children became aware of a situation when it had reached a crisis point. TJ recalled an incident that took place when he was in second grade.

One day, after the lunch break, the students were settling into their seats and the teacher was sitting at her desk. They were all waiting for the afternoon bell to ring. Before the session started, to TJ's surprise, he saw his mother walk into the classroom and approach the teacher. He had no idea why his mother was there.

After the teacher and his mother had a brief discussion, the teacher walked to the front of the class and said, "We are going to have to say good bye to Terry. He will be moving and he will be going to another school."

Not knowing what to say, TJ recalled gathering up his supplies from his desk. He began walking toward the front of the classroom where his mother was waiting. As he walked, he could hear some of the classmates saying good bye. As best as he could, he responded and said his good byes as he walked out of the classroom.

Looking back, TJ recalled walking out and leaving that school for the last time. Thinking about that day still hurts. As a seven year old, he was able to hold his emotions together until he was in the car riding home.

To a mature adult, the situation would appear to be one of irresponsibility, but growing up in this type of family, the feelings continued to be that the parents were the victims. TJ continued to remain loyal to them. However, as time went on, and as TJ matured, he started to look at the situation differently. Some of the excuses and stories began to appear preposterous. For example, when attempting to bring their car payments up to date, the story was that the clerk who prepared a money order for two payments stole the money and the money order was invalid. Really?

TJ's mother would continually have checking accounts closed on her because they were overdrawn. However, she retained the checks and used them to make purchases, even though the accounts were closed. Frequently, there were visitors at the door to collect the money subject to the invalid checks. On one occasion, there was an arrest. The police showed up at the door. Children in these types of situations grow up hating the police. Why not? The police were causing harm to your parents for something that was not their fault. Why couldn't that be understood?

While in high school, TJ was working thirty to forty hours a week. Wanting to help his family, he would give them most of his money—even though both of them were employed full time. One year, TJ filed and received a sizable income tax refund. When it was received, his father suggested that it be kept by the father for safekeeping.

Later, when TJ was going to use the money to buy a car, his father told him that the money was gone a long time ago. The response from his father was expressed in a tone conveying to TJ that he should have known that it would have been gone.

After graduation from high school, his friend, Ron Mason, enrolled at Northern Illinois University in DeKalb, Illinois. Although TJ had intended to do the same, he did not have the funds needed to enroll at that time. His plan was to work a full time job and also a part time job. He expected to save enough money to join Ron by enrolling at Northern Illinois the following year. TJ paid rent to his parents, but tried to keep his money separate for safety reasons.

TJ eventually realized that his parents could not be trusted. He felt that his loyalty had been taken for granted, resulting in him being hurt several times. However, he subsequently had a plan to move on with his life. Even though he suffered by the actions of his parents, he knew that he could deal with it and move on. But another incident occurred that was very upsetting to him.

While at work one day, his sister LeeAnn called him. She was upset and crying. As she explained the situation to him, money had been removed from her bank account by the bank and she did not understand why. As she had done in the past, she was calling her big brother for help with a troubling situation.

TJ immediately called the bank to find out what happened. The bank manager explained to him that their mother had written a check on a closed account. He explained that when he called and spoke with their mother, he was told to take the money out of LeeAnn's bank account. Knowing that this was a pattern that she was engaged in, TJ called his mother for an explanation.

His mother told him that she spoke with LeeAnn, and LeeAnn said it would be okay. TJ asked to speak with LeeAnn, but was told that she was not at home at that time. He then asked his mother to have LeeAnn call him when she returned to the house. No return call was received by TJ.

Later he called LeeAnn to discuss the situation. In his conversation with LeeAnn, she told him that she and their mother had discussed the situation following the contact from the bank. LeeAnn then said that she told the bank officer that it was okay to have the overdrawn funds taken from her account. LeeAnn said that at the time that she called TJ, she had forgotten about the conversation with their mother! What? She lied. His little sister had called him, crying and was very upset. Money was taken out of her account. TJ jumped into action on her behalf. Now he was left hanging, looking like a fool. His mother had actually convinced his sister to subsequently lie to him.

Periodically, TJ was interrupted by some movement or noise during the flight as he was thinking about the past family events. His eventual destination was Chicago, but he would not be staying there very long. In his way of thinking, that was no longer his home. Realistically, he did not want that to be his home.

Later, he reached into his backpack and took out an old letter from his sister, Carla. She was a year and a half younger than TJ. She had married her husband George while TJ was in Afghanistan. He was not able to return for the wedding, but they communicated by mail. He recalls that in planning their wedding, Carla and George were very careful in budgeting their expenses.

Someone had suggested to them that they should only provide beer and wine at the wedding reception. Not providing an assortment of mixed drinks and cocktails would keep the costs down. It seemed like a good idea to them. However, when Carla told their father of their plan, she was met with some resistance. He told them that it sounded pretty chintzy. In other words it would look cheap to the guests. He said his friends, especially his bowling team, would look at him as being a cheapskate.

Being young and naive, Carla and George were subsequently persuaded to offer a full bar to all their wedding reception guests. They both recall their father say that he would take care of the bar tab himself.

Shortly after the wedding dinner, there was a problem. Whether their father had difficulty with math or that he just didn't realize the cost of liquor was not known. Either way, the bartender informed their father that they were running out of money and he was going to have to cut off the liquor unless some additional cash was paid to him. Their father took Carla aside and informed her of the dilemma. He said he did not want to be embarrassed in front of his friends. He was out of money, but suggested that they use the wedding gift money that came with the cards. He promised that he would definitely reimburse them later.

Carla told George of her father's plan. Obviously, George was upset. But he didn't want Carla to be hurt on their wedding day. Although not happy about the situation, he reluctantly agreed to the plan. Carla and her father went to a back room during the reception, carrying the gift envelopes. As they opened each envelope, the names and the amounts were recorded to enable Carla to send out thank you cards. When the process was completed, Carla's father took the cash and paid the bartender to enable him to keep the bar open.

TJ became more angry as he re-read the letter from Carla. He felt that he could always find a way to deal with his parents when he was living with them. Over a period of time he learned to deal with the usual turmoil that was a constant in his family.

But this was different. This was something that was hurting his sister. It was not something that she could just get over. As Carla mentioned, they were promised that the gift money would be reimbursed to them. But it never happened. TJ realized that some things just cannot be repaired.

As the plane began to descend, TJ became more alert. He felt that his physical body would be arriving at his home town destination, but his soul was elsewhere, at a place not even known to himself. He knew that there were only a few things he planned to do. These were indelibly etched in his mind. He knew he had to visit with Ron Mason's parents. They had been like family to him. He was always comfortable in their presence. What that visit would be like at this time he did not know or even want to think about. But it had to be done.

He also needed to see Ron's widow, Stacy. TJ, Ron and Stacy had been students in college together. Referring to Stacy as Ron's widow was so strange to him. Being a widow at such a young age did not seem to fit. The facts were there, but his consciousness was having a difficult time accepting it.

TJ's ultimate goal was to get to California. That was something that he and Ron had talked about often. The seeds were planted when Ron went on vacation with his parents during his early high school years. Ron would talk about the mountains, the deserts and the ocean. In fact he talked about that all the time. TJ remembers Ron telling him that he told his family that, after seeing the mountains, he knew he was no longer in Illinois.

Whether that was going to be just a trip for the two of them or an ultimate destination was not really discussed. Just getting there was what they always talked about. Ron discussed that goal so often that TJ seemed to formally accept the same goal as a desired destination. Either way, it was something that they were going to do together. Now TJ felt that he had to complete that mission to honor Ron's memory.

On the way to California, TJ would make one other stop. He planned to see one of their Marine buddies, Tom Harris. TJ, Ron and Tom had spent much time together in Afghanistan. Tom seemed to be a good fit along with the two of them. Tom was discharged a year before TJ. He lived on a farm with his family in Kansas. On his way to California, TJ would briefly stop to see Tom.

Other than those contacts, TJ had no other plans to see anyone. Nothing else was necessary for him to do.

The plane landed at O'Hare Airport in Chicago. The greeting party consisted of TJ's parents and two of his sisters that were still living at home. By most accounts, it would be a happy homecoming. His family was thankful that he was coming home after being honorably discharged from the Marines.

Although TJ was coming home, he knew that he would not be there very long. These thoughts were not known to anyone at the homecoming. He refused to think much about any plans at that time. After he gathered his baggage, the family left the airport and drove him to their home in Brookfield, a suburban town in the area. TJ would stay there for a few days until his married sister, Carla, and her husband, George, drove up from Joliet the following Sunday.

TJ's mother said she planned to have a welcome home party for his family and friends to give him a homecoming that he so richly deserved. She planned to invite several of her friends, telling TJ that they wanted so badly to meet him.

Without intending to hurt his mother's feelings, TJ asked her if she could delay any welcome back party for a little while until he could get adjusted to being back home. Realistically, he didn't want a party. Telling her to delay it seemed like an easy way to ease himself into the avoidance of seeing a lot of people, many of whom he had never known. His mother had a habit of inviting many of what she expressed as "close friends" to her home. Realistically, she may have only met many of them only a few weeks earlier.

For now, he just asked her to give him some time to get adjusted. He knew that she didn't understand, but she agreed to do that for him. TJ's father heard all of the conversations regarding a party, but said nothing. TJ expected that lack of response from his father. He was used to it from past experiences. It was his father's way of dealing with whatever came up in their lives.

The day after his arrival, TJ rented a car. He needed to be alone in his thoughts as he would drive around the area. This was an area that he had lived in for most of his life, but he was no longer feeling any attachment to it. Everything seemed strange to him. He felt that he did not belong there. He wasn't sure why. It was just strange to him. Maybe this is the adjustment that he was told by the military counselors that he might experience following his discharge. They said it might take a while for him to adjust. They also told him that there were many re-enlistments of soldiers following a period of attempted re-adjustments to civilian life.

TJ needed to rent a car because the pickup truck that he owned was in Joliet at the home of his sister and brother-in-law. After their arrival to see TJ on Sunday, he would go back with them to get his truck. He was told by his mother that his sister brought it to their home in Joliet because there was not enough room at the location where his parents currently lived. His parents continued a pattern of moving to various residences over the years. As he knew, this was a familiar scenario to him from past years. Although being familiar with that pattern, he never understood it. They both worked and had good incomes, but something always seemed amiss.

Driving around made him feel like a stranger in the area. He just had no desire to connect with anyone from the past. Other than the obligations to see Ron's parents, Stacy and Tom Harris, he just did not want to connect with anyone. He just convinced himself that he needed nobody.

TJ's sister, Carla, and her husband George arrived on Sunday. It was good to see her and to meet her husband for the first time. On Sunday night, TJ planned to ride back to Joliet with Carla and George where he could retrieve his truck. TJ was reminded again by his mother that she needed to schedule the homecoming party for all of her friends that were looking forward to meeting with him.

TJ again told his mother that after he picked up his truck and returned from Joliet, he would have a better handle on his schedule. She asked when that would be. He told her that he just didn't know. However, unbeknownst to her, when he left with Carla and George, he took all of his belongings with him—not that he had much.

On the trip to Joliet, TJ was informed by Carla that she and their mother had not talked to each other for several months. That fact was concealed pretty well during that Sunday after Carla and George had arrived in Brookfield. TJ asked what had caused this current falling out between them. Carla and George looked at each other, and nodded.

Carla looked at TJ and said, "Believe it or not, it all got started over your pickup truck."

"What?"

"Our mother was looking for the title to your truck."

"But you have the truck, right," inquired TJ.

"Yes. George told me that we'd better get the truck and keep it at our place," explained Carla.

"Good, because I have the title," responded TJ.

George said nothing, but only listened as he drove.

Carla went on, "Terry, I mean TJ, I think you know her well enough that she could find some way to get a duplicate title. If she had it, she could easily forge your signature on the title."

"Okay to call me Terry," said TJ. "I still respond to that. But what was she going to do with the title? Sell the truck?"

"We had a big argument about the situation. She told me that she would only use it as collateral for a loan. She said that you would understand and she was sure you would agree to it."

TJ sat quietly listening.

"I told her that if that was what she wanted to do, then she should write to you and ask you. That's when we stopped talking to each other."

"Well, thank you. Both of you," TJ said softly.

"I hate talking about our mother like that," explained Carla. "I just wish I didn't have to say those things, but we know it's true"

"I know," acknowledged TJ.

"I wrote to you about what happened at our wedding and how our gifts of money were used to pay for the liquor, right? That was because Dad said it would have put him in an awkward situation with all of his friends," Carla summarized.

"Yes," said TJ

"It really put us in a bind," Carla went on. "No honeymoon. We should have stuck to our guns and offered only beer and wine. If those lushes had to have their mixed drinks, they could have paid for the drinks themselves. George told me that he saw several glasses that were half full and left on tables. Why not? All they had to do was just go up to the bar and get another drink. They didn't have to pay for it. We did."

"That's true," commented TJ.

"I don't think George and I will ever forget that," Carla went on. "We might have felt differently if we were reimbursed as Dad had promised. But that never happened."

TJ said nothing further, knowing that there was nothing else that could be added to her thoughts or words.

Chapter Two
Moving On

TJ stayed overnight at the home of Carla and George. The next morning, George left early to go to work. TJ woke up to the smell of coffee. As he laid in bed, his mind strayed back to the Marines and to Afghanistan—memories of the time served with Ron Mason. His thoughts then drifted back to the years when they were in school together. Those years appeared to have gone by so fast. At least that's how it was appearing at this time. He reminded himself that nothing lasts forever. However, he wished that life, as he recalled, had not ended so abruptly.

To put himself in a better frame of mind, he would reminisce about various events in a sequential manner. It started when they first met in high school in Brookfield, Illinois. Then he would transition his thoughts to the time they were together at Northern Illinois University. They were always together. The only difference between the two of them was that Ron had gotten married six months into his third year at Northern Illinois University. He married Stacy, his long time girlfriend from high school. She was also attending Northern Illinois.

The trip through his memories included their time in the Marines. Not all memories were fun and games. Boot camp in the Marines did not fall into that kind of category. But being together and the camaraderie that was developed in the Marines became something special to both of them. Then he realized that what he remembered from the past existed only in a vanishing world

His thoughts then turned to the present time and his current situation. Thanks to George, he still had a pickup truck. He knew, as George knew, the truck would likely have been gone if his mother had time to carry out her plans. It would not have been the first time that he would have taken a loss because of his family.

TJ always did what he could do to help his family. While working a part time job and going to high school, most of the money earned was given to his family. It just seemed automatic to him to do what he could to help out. He was too close to the situation to look at it objectively. Both of his parents worked, but had nothing to show for it.

TJ chuckled to himself as he thought about how he had previously convinced himself that they were always victims. Things always happened to them that prevented them from getting ahead. When one grows up in that kind of environment, one tends to buy into it. TJ used to feel that he was a victim also. How naive he was during those early years

As he matured, he came in contact with other people and other families. Ron Mason's family was one that made TJ realize that all families were not like the one that he came from. As difficult as it was to come to grips with reality, he had to be honest with himself. In his best interests, he felt that he had to avoid any future contacts with his family. He had to rid himself of that toxic relationship.

When his sister Carla realized that TJ was awake, she started to make breakfast. Drawn by the smell of the coffee, TJ got out of bed and headed toward the kitchen.

"Good morning," he said to Carla.

"Good morning," responded Carla. "I didn't want to wake you up."

"You didn't. The coffee did. That's always a good way for me to start the day."

As TJ sat down at the kitchen table, he looked up at Carla and said, "Thanks again for taking care of my truck. I appreciate you looking out for me."

"Actually, George was the one who insisted on making that move. Maybe I was too close to the situation and did not see what could have happened, you know, being part of the family. But George put things in motion and convinced me that we had to protect the truck for you."

"Well, thanks again to both of you."

"Looking back, I'm afraid that if our mother had the title and the truck, it would have been gone by the time you came back," explained Carla.

"Well, I have it now."

"Do you have any plans on what you might want to do, you know, now that you're back home?" inquired Carla.

"No," TJ answered, "but one thing for sure, I don't want to be part of any homecoming party. You know how it would be. Our mother would invite all her friends, none of which I know."

"I know," concurred Carla.

"She tells me that her friends are all dying to meet me. And then she tells those friends that I am looking forward to meeting them. I'm just all too familiar with that scenario," explained TJ. "I just don't want any part of it."

"Of course it would be an opportunity to see some of your old friends," offered Carla.

"I don't feel I have any old friends. And I don't feel that I need any friends at this time in my life."

Carla just listened, but added nothing further.

"One thing I have to do is to look up Stacy, Ron's widow," responded TJ. "I still can't believe those words are coming out of my mouth. Widow? Growing up, that always applied to someone's spouse after the individual got older, got sick and then died. You would send an obituary card to the widow or the widower. But Stacy is only twenty one or twenty two years old. It just doesn't fit."

"I know. It's really sad."

"From what I understand, after school, she got a job right in town I guess she lives and works right there in DeKalb," said TJ. "After that I feel that I would like to visit with Ron's parents. They were always so good to me. They even helped me with my tuition when I thought I might have to drop out of school. I haven't seen them since Ron and I left for deployment overseas."

"I'm starting to understand how you must feel at this time," Carla reasoned. "Seeing his parents seems appropriate."

"Actually, I'm not looking forward to seeing either one of them," reasoned TJ. "It's not going to be very comfortable for me. I have no idea what to say, but it has to be done. Sometimes you just want to leave the past in the past."

"Maybe you don't need to say anything," said Carla. "Just being there is important."

"That reminds me of something. When we were in boot camp, I found a poem that someone had written. It speaks to not wanting to know about the future as it relates to the people you knew. Believe it or not, the consensus was that it was written by a drill sergeant during World War II," explained TJ. "The author is not identified. The poem was signed as Anonymous. After reading it and thinking about it, I think I understand the feelings he had. I have a folder that I have used for saving various clippings and articles over the years."

"You've always saved things that way," commented Carla. "I remember you had saved various clippings, going back to high school. You even had expressions you saved from a book you read by Norman Vincent Peale."

Yes," responded TJ. "His book was *The Power of Positive Thinking*. I used to read it when I was down, or kind of depressed. It kept me going. His book made me feel more positive about things. It got me through some of those tough times. Anyway, here, let me show you the poem"

"But why would an author not want anybody to know that he wrote something?" commented Carla.

"Well, as I was saying, we think it was written by a drill sergeant," said TJ. "He probably didn't want to identify himself because the wrong people might think he was too soft. You know, the superior officers want the drill sergeants to be as hard as nails. In boot camp, if the troops hate the drill sergeant, then he was probably doing a good job."

"That's probably true," responded Carla. That's what I have been told before, and of course, that's what is shown all the time in the movies we see."

"Yes, that's the reality of it. You need to show toughness to develop that type of soldier," explained TJ

"I guess that's true," agreed Carla.

"Anyway, here, let me show you the poem."

<u>TRAINER OF THE TROOPS</u>

We welcomed you, you look so young,
We trained you to defend, to protect,
We fed you, we clothed you, we equipped you,
We send you away, not knowing your fate.
Will you be back to fulfill your dreams? We hope so.
But we don't know, we just don't want to know.
Will you raise your children; teach them right from wrong?
Life will be yours; you can shape the future.
Some will be back to fulfill their dreams, others will not.
Who will be back, who will not?
We don't know, We just don't want to know.
Let us dream, because in our dreams, you will all be back,
To fulfill your lives, but please don't tell us who, because
We don't want to know. We just don't want to know.

Anonymous

"That's really interesting," Carla commented.

"Yes," answered TJ. "I don't think it would have won a Pulitzer Prize, but it certainly gets his message across. And I understand his feelings. You don't want to know the results of some of the people you knew. It might be too painful," explained TJ.

"I think it says a lot," offered Carla

"I'm sure that just writing it satisfied his need to express it," said TJ.

That night when Carla's husband George came home from work, the three of them had dinner together. During dinner, TJ had told George of his plans to visit Stacy in DeKalb and also Ron's parents in Brookfield.

It was at that time that George informed TJ that Ron's father no longer was on the police force in Brookfield and did not live in the area. George seemed to have a great awareness of people and situations regarding what was going on. He was good for Carla, after coming from what she and TJ felt was a dysfunctional family.

As George explained the circumstances, it seems that shortly after Ron was killed in Afghanistan, unfortunately, Ron's father and mother had separated. Subsequently, Ron's father left the Brookfield police force and became the Sheriff in Kendall County, Illinois.

Ironically, Kendall County was near DeKalb. TJ decided to visit Ron's father in Kendall County and then go to see Stacy in DeKalb after that. As he had explained to Carla, these were two of the visits that he felt committed to make.

Chapter Three

Ron Mason's Parents

The news of the separation of Ron's parents was very upsetting to TJ. They had always appeared to be a close family. TJ realized that the loss of his friend was difficult, but it had to be devastating to Ron's parents, especially being their only child.

Ron's dad had always been a special person to TJ. He remembered how he was always available to give TJ a ride home after he and Ron were involved in some school activities together, such as games or practices. That was a complete contrast to the way his own father handled similar situations.

One incident relating to TJ's father stood out in his mind. TJ had planned to try out for the school baseball team. He had discussed and arranged for his father to pick him up after school on his father's way home from work Other than stopping at the school, there was little inconvenience for his father. TJ's father did pick him up at school. However, on the way home, his father asked him, "How long will this be going on?" That comment remained in TJ's memory.

Some time later, TJ was working on a project with Ron at Ron's home on a Saturday. When they had completed the project, TJ needed a ride home. However, he was reluctant to call his father, being concerned that his father would balk at coming to pick him up. He told Ron that his father was not at home because he had to work overtime. The story was a fabrication.

Ron asked his father if he could drive TJ home. No problem. Consider it done seemed to be his father's attitude for Ron's friends. TJ lived a little out of the way, but still, no problem for Ron's dad.

As the car rounded the corner and entered the block where he lived, TJ could see that his father's car was in the driveway of their home. TJ immediately offered, "Oh, my dad must have gotten home earlier from work than he thought."

As he thought about it in later years, he realized that Ron's dad probably was aware of the situation. But knowing Ron's dad, he didn't concern himself with those details. He was taking Ron's friend home, and that's all that mattered to him. TJ never forgot that. Ron's dad may have even felt bad that TJ had to come up with a story to protect his father. Because of times like that, TJ felt that it was important to stop by and see Ron's dad.

TJ knew that there was a strong relationship between Ron and his dad. Ron's dad had been in the Marines. He and Ron had engaged in many discussions regarding the Marines. It seemed to TJ that Ron was destined to follow in his dad's footsteps and eventually join the Marines at some point.

As his dad talked about the Marines, Ron always remembered his dad telling him that once you're a Marine, you're always a Marine. Not that his dad had intended Ron to join the Marines, but Ron could see the impact it had on his dad, and that meant a lot to him.

After completion of his third year at Northern Illinois, Ron decided that he wanted to enlist in the Marines. Despite all the discussions between Ron and his dad regarding the Marines, the decision came as a surprise to Ron's dad, especially at that time. That's because Ron had not completed his college education.

Ron's mother was not happy at all with his decision. She tried to dissuade Ron from joining. She could see that he developed a strong interest in the Marines. However, realizing that she would not be able to change his ultimate desire, she tried to convince him to first complete his education. She told him that getting his degree would give him a greater advantage when he enlisted.

Having been recently married to Stacy added to the element of surprise for both of his parents. TJ didn't know what Stacy's feelings were about Ron's decision, but it seemed to him that Stacy had always supported Ron in whatever he chose to do. It could be that Ron and Stacy had been discussing the decision for some time, but kept their private thoughts to themselves.

Ron's decision to join the Marines also had an impact on TJ. Although he had completed two years at Northern Illinois, it became apparent to him that he would not have the necessary funds to carry him through a third year. In fact, Ron's dad had loaned TJ money for tuition to complete his second year. TJ didn't ask for a loan. Word of his financial dilemma was conveyed to Ron's dad by Ron. The savings that TJ had accumulated in a joint savings account with his parents seemed to have evaporated. He was told that it was due to an emergency that his parents encountered.

Faced with his financial situation and the uncertainties in planning for the future, TJ decided that it would be a good move for him to also join the Marines along with Ron. Realistically, TJ was focused more on what he was leaving, as opposed to looking toward the future. He rationalized that his new destination would be a good change in his life.

TJ called the Kendall County Sheriff's Office and asked to speak to Sheriff Mason. As anticipated, he had to go through a few layers of red tape before Mr. Mason came on the telephone.

"TJ, how are you?"

"Good. I just thought I'd stop by and say hello."

"Of course."

"I know you're busy. I won't take much of your time," offered TJ.

"Nonsense. Are you in the area?"

"Yes I am," responded TJ.

"Then come on over, if you know where I'm at."

TJ drove over to the Sheriff's Office. He walked in and gave his name to the receptionist and informed her that he was there to see Sheriff Mason.

"Oh, yes. He's been expecting you."

Within a couple of minutes, Mr. Mason came into the lobby. He walked over to TJ and gave him a hug. "Good to see you. Let's go to lunch. Or dinner. What time is it anyway?"

"I don't want to intrude on your time," said TJ.

"Come on. We all have to eat."

That said, the two of them walked out of the front door and approached a sheriff's vehicle. Sheriff Mason drove to a restaurant and the two went in. As can be anticipated, the Sheriff was greeted by the host who led them to a private table in the back of the restaurant.

The two of them had a good discussion about sports and various news items of the day. Later, after they finished their dinner, Mr. Mason became more serious. He told TJ that losing their son, their only child, was devastating to both himself and Mrs. Mason.

Whenever they would be together, Ron would come up in their conversation. It became inevitable no matter what they were doing. It just could not be avoided. They just could not get past the sadness of the loss.

After many discussions, they decided to separate. Mrs. Mason still lived in Brookfield and continued to work at her same job. Mr. Mason said he feels that they were still in love with each other, but a change was needed for each one of them. At least, that's how they both felt. Who knows if that was the right thing to do. But it seemed right at the time. Maybe things might change in the future he concluded.

TJ continued to listen to Ron's dad as he tried to explain his situation. He knew what it was like to lose his best friend. Now he was hearing about the impact it had on Ron's parents.

"But what about you? What are you going to do now that you're back home?" Mr. Mason inquired.

"I really don't know. I'm planning to head west. To California actually," answered TJ. "I did promise to stop and see one of our buddies who lives in Kansas. During the trip west I plan to stop by and see him."

"California. You know after we vacationed there, that's all Ron would talk about," added Mr. Mason.

"I know. We talked about that a lot while we were in Afghanistan," said TJ. "We discussed taking a trip there when we got back home."

"Will you be traveling there alone?"

"Yes, that's my plan," answered TJ.

"Be careful. Don't drive if you get tired. Keep your eyes and ears open. There are a lot of strange people out there," advised Mr. Mason. "There I go. Sounding like a cop. I guess I can't get away from it."

TJ just smiled.

"Let's get back to the station. I'll give you a tour,"

After getting back to the Sheriff's Office, he did give TJ a complete tour of the facility. Then the two of them went back to his private office.

"Here's what I'm going to do," said Mr. Mason. "I'm am going to deputize you and make you part of this office."

"What? Really? But I'm planning to head west to California," responded a surprised and confused TJ.

"I know. So you're on leave."

TJ just grinned.

"You're going to have to be armed if your a deputy," he explained. "That will give me the satisfaction that you are going to be able to protect yourself," explained Mr. Mason. "That is essential for your own safety.

"Can you do that?" asked TJ.

"Of course I can. I'm the sheriff. Maybe it's all those years in law enforcement, but I never went anywhere without being armed. You know, for your protection it's necessary. As police officers, we have always been armed whether we're on duty or off duty. It's done under the guise that we may be needed to help other law enforcement personnel when needed. But that's all bullshit. No police department wants some unknown cop walking into their operation and telling them that he's a cop from a nearby town and he can assist them. You can understand that they don't want that kind of intrusion. It would create all kinds of confusion. Realistically, we all just feel better when we're armed. We do it for our own protection."

"I do understand what you're saying," concurred TJ. "I guess I never looked at it that way."

"Here, let me deputize you and I'll get you the equipment and accessories that you'll need," said Sheriff Mason.

In addition to the pistol, ammunition and the holster, TJ was given a special holster that secured the pistol around the calf of his leg. He was told that one never knows when this might be needed. Ron's dad did express his paranoia, but rationalized that it has kept him alive all these years.

Before they finished their discussion, TJ expressed his appreciation for the tuition loan that he received from Ron's dad.

"My pleasure. The debt has been paid. Being a good friend of Ron's through the years was payment enough for me."

TJ didn't know what to say. He started to feel emotional.

Sheriff Mason just changed the subject, "I think you'll like California."

After saying their farewells, TJ left the Sheriff's Station as a member of the Sheriff's Department of Kendall County. He put his pistol in the glove compartment and put the holsters under the seat on the passenger side.

Chapter Four

Visit with Stacy

After TJ left the Sheriff's Office, he drove toward DeKalb, his next designated stop. He needed to contact Stacy. As he had been told, she still lived in that area. But it was too late to see her that night, or even to call her. He was not prepared, or in the proper frame of mind, to make a call at that time. He needed to think about what he would say to her.

It was kind of ironic that TJ was driving his pickup truck with a pistol in the glove department. After leaving Afghanistan, he had no thoughts of ever carrying a gun again. However, he would honor Mr. Mason's suggestion that he protect himself, but it is unlikely that it would ever be used. But he'll keep it.

Being familiar with DeKalb from his days as a student, TJ knew his way around. He was looking for a small, out of the way motel, where he would spend the night. In doing so, he was hoping that he would not run across anybody that he knew. He just didn't feel like talking.

He drove to an area on the outskirts of town. He was looking for a small motel. Seeing a "Vacancy" sign at one location, he decided to register there. He parked his truck and entered the reception area. There he was greeted by a middle aged lady who walked slowly up to the counter.

She asked him, "How many in your party?"

"Just myself. Two nights," he responded.

"Looking for anyplace in particular?" she inquired.

"No, just checking out the campus," he said.

As he responded, he kind of looked away, conveying a message that he did not feel like having any conversation. In response, she gave him the check-in card for him to fill out and record his vehicle description and license plate number. After completing that task and paying for the two nights, he was given the key and directions to where the room was located and where he would need to park his vehicle. He turned and left with a simple, "Thank you."

The room was small, as expected—bed, dresser, television and a couple of chairs. No doubt, a Gideon Bible was in the dresser drawer.

He turned on the television. Paying little attention to the television programming, TJ just laid himself on top of the bed and soon went into a deep sleep.

The next morning TJ awoke early, not knowing whether it was the TV that seemed to nudge him awake, or the daylight that was attempting to pass through the drapes. Despite the cause for his awakening, he felt that it was time to get up. Shortly thereafter, he was in the shower.

He left the motel, and drove around looking for a place to have breakfast. A coffee shop that he remembered from his student days was nearby. As he entered, he asked for a table for one. When none was available, he said the counter would be okay.

As he sat at the counter, again he was hoping that he didn't see any familiar faces. He just didn't feel like talking, especially giving an account of his prior whereabouts since leaving school.

Fortunately for TJ, all of the faces were those of strangers. After breakfast, he drove around the area. Many of the campus buildings brought back memories. He was a little surprised at some of the changes. There seemed to be new buildings and several buildings under construction. He realized that some of the locations he had remembered were now gone. It may have seemed like progress to some, but it was probably the loss of memories for others.

After a while, TJ told himself that he needed to call Stacy. He kept telling himself that she was the widow of his best friend. It was going to be difficult. What were the right words to say. He was ambivalent about talking to her. It would be so easy to just forget about doing so, and just drive out of town. But how could he just walk away? After thinking further about it, he knew that he couldn't live with that scenario.

Eventually, TJ drove his pickup truck into a parking lot. After stopping in a parking space, he sat for a few minutes. Taking out his cell phone, he dialed Stacy's number. Maybe it would just ring. It might be disconnected. Who knows? Then TJ heard Stacy's familiar voice say, "Hello."

"Hi, Stacy. It's TJ."

"Hello. How are you?"

"Fine. I was in town and I thought I'd give you a call."

"Well, good. It's good hearing your voice. You say you're in town? Here in DeKalb?"

"Yes. I didn't want to intrude, but I wanted to say hello before I left."

"I'm glad you called. Will we be able to see each other?"

"Sure," responded TJ.

"I'm at work now, but if you have the time, maybe I can see you later," she offered

"Let me take you out to dinner tonight after work. That is, if you have the time and if you're available," he asked.

"Yes, I would be. Let me give you my address. Would six be good for you?" she asked him.

"Yes."

Stacy then gave TJ her address. "I'll see you at six."

TJ went back to his motel to wait a couple of hours before he would take Stacy to dinner. He thought he'd lay on the bed and watch television. He had a few hours to kill, but told himself to be careful not to fall asleep.

TJ dressed casually, but presentable for his dinner with Stacy. He gave himself a sufficient amount of time to drive to her apartment, not wanting to get caught up with any unexpected traffic delays. Despite some mild traffic, he was in the area well in advance of six o'clock. No problem. He would just park a few blocks from her apartment so he could be there on time.

Allowing enough time, he arrived at Stacy's front door at precisely six o'clock. Moments after ringing the doorbell, the door opened and Stacy appeared with her usual smile. The two of them reached out and gave each other a hug. She was very pretty, with brown hair brushing her shoulders and beautiful brown eyes. And that captivating smile completed the special picture that he remembered.

"You look good," she said through her smile.

"And you look as great as I always remembered," TJ responded.

"You're flattering me," she said.

"I hope you're hungry," he stated.

"Yes. There's a nice place a couple of miles from here," she offered. "Not a sports bar with fifty games going on all at once. It's a nice place with background music. We won't have to shout at each other to be heard."

"Sounds good."

The two of them left Stacy's apartment and walked to TJ's pickup truck. Stacy directed TJ to the restaurant.

"This isn't valet parking is it?" TJ asked.

"No. It's self parking. A nice restaurant, but no tuxedo required," she explained with a grin.

As they entered the restaurant, they were led to a table. TJ could see that there were very few patrons in the restaurant. Being a weekday, it probably was not as occupied as it may have been on a weekend. Stacy ordered a glass of wine and TJ ordered a beer. After a couple of rounds, they ordered dinner. They had a nice discussion during dinner. Sometimes it became a little emotional, thinking about the past when they were in school with Ron

The three of them, along with TJ's dates, had engaged in a variety of activities, many of which were related to college events. Although Ron and Stacy were constant companions, it seemed that TJ had a different date each time. Ron and Stacy seemed to hit it off very quickly after they met at high school. It seemed to everyone that they were destined to always be together.

After dinner, TJ and Stacy drove back to her apartment. TJ got out and walked her up to the door of her apartment. At the door, Stacy asked, "Would you like to come in for a bit?"

"I would like that," answered TJ.

"I have some beer, but probably only lite beer."

"That's fine. That works for me," answered TJ.

The two of them continued to discuss a variety of topics. TJ consumed two beers, while Stacy nursed one beer during that time. TJ then noticed that Stacy's mood began to change.

"It has been so difficult for me," she expressed to TJ. "You know Ron and I were always together, in whatever we did."

"I know that," TJ said in agreement.

"When he was gone, I dealt with that," she went on. "It was a difficult adjustment for me. But what kept me going was that I convinced myself that it would only be for a certain period of time."

TJ just sat and listened.

"That's how it was. Convincing myself that he would be back kept me going each day. Then the shocking news came. After that, you wake up each day and the first thought is that you had a dream. Probably your mind playing tricks on you and just giving you some wishful thinking. Reality follows quickly. And you realize that nothing will change."

"I wish things could be different," offered TJ.

"There's so much I miss. Sometimes just simple things. Having a hand touch my shoulder, being held, feeling his warm body next to mine."

"I feel so bad for you," said TJ. "We all feel the loss, but I know that this is so hard on you. I hear what you're saying. It's all so painful."

Then Stacy got up from her chair and said, "I'll be right back," as she walked out of the living room.

TJ sat up in his chair, thinking she probably went to the washroom. He started thinking that he probably should get going.

A few minutes later, Stacy came back in the living room. she was wearing a white robe.

She looked at TJ and said, "I really do need to be held. I miss that so much."

TJ got up off the couch and walked over to Stacy, put his arms around her and gave her a hug. She hugged him back. Stacy then opened her robe, showing her full body. At the same time she reached out and clutched TJ's hand. Holding his hand, she led him to the couch.

As they sat on the couch, she began to unbutton TJ's shirt. He helped by taking off his shirt. The two of them embraced. They began to lie on the couch.

Then Stacy suddenly stiffened and sat up. "I can't do this. I just can't do this now. Maybe I'll never be able to do this again. I'm sorry."

TJ sat up and said, "That's okay. It's okay. Nothing happened."

'I'm sorry. I must be crazy," she explained.

"It's okay," repeated TJ. "No, you're not crazy. We're friends. Nothing happened. You didn't do anything wrong."

"I'm sorry. This was my fault."

"No. Nobody's fault," TJ tried to assure her. "We've never been through a loss like this. But don't blame yourself."

"I just feel bad."

"No. It's okay. Really. We're good friends, and we're doing our best to deal with a loss," TJ tried his best to console her.

TJ got up and wrapped the robe around Stacy. "We'll get through this," expressed TJ, trying to assure Stacy. At the same time, he was trying to assure himself as well.

"I really should get going."

"Okay," said Stacy. "Friends. Thank you for your understanding. And being a friend," she said with a smile.

TJ smiled back and gave Stacy a hug. "Good bye. Until we meet again."

And then he left. As he drove away in his truck, he thought about Stacy and the difficulty that she was going through. Realistically, TJ was thinking that they would likely never see each other again. As he was heading back to the motel, he felt exhausted. The next day, he would be heading west.

Chapter Five

Dejection and Despair

The next morning TJ checked out of the motel. Not realizing he would fall into a deep sleep, he almost missed the noon checkout requirement. As he drove away from the motel he felt that he had no destination at that moment.

After driving down the road, he remembered a park that was near the area. He drove his truck into the park and drove around until he found one of the designated parking areas. Ironically, his was the only vehicle there. Then again, it was a weekday.

He just sat there in his truck. Nothing seemed to be going right for him. He hadn't anticipated the activities that took place with Stacy. He began blaming himself for the way the events had transpired.

She was Ron's wife— the wife of his best friend. How could he allow himself to be in that situation? Then rationalizing, he blamed it on the emotions that the two of them were feeling. Maybe he should never have stopped to see her. But that would not be right. He felt that he had an obligation to see her.

He started thinking that it would have been better if he had maintained control and stopped any emotional entanglement. He could have just told Stacy that it was not the right thing to do. Had he acted in that manner, they would have both come to their senses and acted properly. That would have been right for him. And probably the best for Stacy.

But as he thought further about avoiding that difficult encounter, his mind brought him to the feelings of Stacy. What if he had acted as he was now thinking. Yes, it would have been proper. But would Stacy have felt rejected? Here was a young attractive woman who recently lost her husband. She was feeling the natural emotions of a young woman and the need to be loved. How would she deal with a rejection? There were no easy answers.

Occasionally, a car would drive by. Otherwise, it was quiet. TJ continued to just sit in his truck, thinking about everything. He felt disgusted. He was disgusted with his life and everything in his life. He hated everything—everything and everybody.

He thought of the sequential events that he had experienced during and since Afghanistan. Since his return from the service, his life did not seem to be getting any better. Was that enough to warrant one to end a life? He continued to deliberate about the past and the future. He seemed to be convincing himself that there was no hope for him to go on. But then he thought about his promise to stop and see one of his buddies on his trip west.

Going to California? Ron loved his trip to California with his family. He loved it so much so that he and TJ promised each other that when they got back from their time in Afghanistan, they would take a trip to California together. In a way, he felt an obligation to complete the trip. But then again, he was alone. Ron was no longer here. Did he still have that obligation? He was tired of commitments. He was tired of always trying to do the right thing. Does he owe anybody anything anymore. Looking back, where did that way of thinking get him? The result seemed to be that everyone would take advantage of him.

After a few moments, he unlocked the glove compartment. He reached in, took out the pistol and closed the glove compartment. For what seemed to be an eternity, he just held the pistol on his lap. The weapon was given to him by Mr. Mason for his protection. Did he need it for protection?

He began to think about something he had heard and also read about. The expression was to always save one bullet. Pilots in wartime situations would feel that way. In the event that they would be captured, and be concerned about being tortured, they would always save one bullet. To them that was the right course of action. Here he was, torturing himself. It had to stop. He could stop it.

TJ lifted his pistol and put the barrel of the gun against his head. It felt like he was in a trance. He kept thinking that he could stop the pain. It was the answer he needed.

Just then he heard the voice of a little girl yelling, "Daddy, Daddy, look a swing."

A surprised TJ lowered the pistol to his lap and looked around to see where that voice was coming from. Then he saw a little girl riding her bicycle. She stopped at a nearby swing set. Following closely behind her on another bicycle was what appeared to be her father. By the time the father stopped his bicycle, the little girl was already sitting on the swing. She was waiting for her father to give her a push. She was so excited.

TJ continued to hold the pistol on his lap. After a few moments, he opened the glove compartment and put the pistol away.

"Not today, TJ," he said to himself. "Not today."

There was no way that he was going to destroy a moment of joy for that little girl and her Daddy. He started his pickup truck and drove out of the park.

Chapter Six

A Needed Timeout

After leaving the park, TJ was feeling hungry. It was mid afternoon and he realized he hadn't eaten anything all day. He decided to stop and get something to eat. He located a nearby drive through fast food restaurant.

As soon as his order was picked up, he looked for a shady spot to park. Finding one, he shut down his truck and began to eat his meal. As he ate, he tried to clear his head of the recent events. While sitting in his truck, he could see a billboard across the street that read:

DON'T BUY A PET—ADOPT ONE
WE HAVE THAT WARM HEARTED COMPANION
NEEDING A PERMANENT FRIEND FOR LIFE

The message made TJ smile. He had convinced himself that he did not need a friend. He'd been through that scenario before It was too painful losing one. As he continued to eat his sandwich, he realized that he never thought about a dog as a friend. His curiosity was starting to get the best of him. He looked again at the billboard—A PERMANENT FRIEND FOR LIFE.

He recalled a news item that he had clipped and saved. As Carla had mentioned to him, he always had a habit of saving various newspaper clippings and quotes that were of interest to him and kept them in a folder. Back in October 2016, there was a news item about a house fire in Spokane, Washington. For some reason, that he could not explain to himself at the time, he had saved the item from the newspaper. It seemed to strike a chord with him that was not easily forgotten. He reached into the back seat to find his backpack and pulled out his folder. He thumbed through the folder to find the newspaper clipping that he remembered saving. When he found it, he took it out and read it again:

Boy's body found with toy, dog

A toddler who died in a house fire
in Spokane, Wash., was found with his
dog and teddy bear next to him and
authorities believe the dog tried to protect
the boy, a fire spokesman said. The dog, a
terrier mixed breed, also died in the fire.

Maybe what he retained from the article was the theme of loyalty. Through his military training, one develops loyalties within the Marine brotherhood. Although he still felt that he didn't need a friend, he wasn't thinking of that kind of friend. Previously, he did recall reading about the loyalty of dogs in the military. It probably was due to the loyalty shown by the boy's dog that convinced him to keep the news clipping.

However he was not convinced that he wanted to take that route. He didn't really need a dog. But he thought that the message on the billboard was very persuasive.

He picked up his cell phone and looked up the facility. It was not that far from where he was parked. He decided to drive by the facility. When he arrived at the location, it looked as if it might be closing. Few vehicles were in the parking lot. He parked his truck and thought he would check it out. At least he could see what their hours were. He walked to the door and saw that it was still open. He entered, but didn't see any attendant. Then a lady, appearing to be in her fifties or sixties, came out of an office from the back of the area.

"Can I help you," she asked.

"Yes," responded TJ. "I was in the area and I saw your ad on a billboard. I thought I would stop by and take a look."

"Were you looking for a pet?"

"No, but a friend of mine said he might be interested in getting a pet and I thought I would check it out for him," he fabricated.

"Okay, let's take a look," she suggested. "That way you can let your friend know what we have here."

He followed her. As he walked through the aisles, he could see that there were all types of dogs and cats. Some were together in one caged area while others were in separate cages.

As he walked through, he noticed one large sized dog with dark fur. For some reason, he and the dog made eye contact with each other. He continued to walk down the aisle, looking at the dogs. He then looked back at the one he made eye contact with. It was still looking at him.

After turning the corner and heading toward the next aisle, TJ asked, "What kind of dog is that, back in the middle of the aisle?"

"Oh, that one is an Irish Setter," she responded. "They're really popular, and good with children."

"I'm familiar with Irish Setters. But I was talking about that large one with the dark fur," he inquired.

"That one is a male. It's approximately three to four years old," she responded. "At least, that's what the veterinarian thinks."

"What's his story?"

"Oh, that's an interesting one," she went on. "I really didn't know what type of breed that it was. We asked Dr. Thillens, who is the veterinarian affiliated with our shelter. Believe it or not, he considers himself to be a canine historian."

"Really," said TJ, following along.

"Yes. And he identified him as an Anatolian Shepherd. He said the breed goes back to 2000 B.C. They were used to guard livestock in Turkey, I believe he said. Apparently, they were also used for protecting the family from outsiders. He added that they are a very intelligent breed."

"And someone gave him up?"

"Actually he was found in a vacant area described as a homeless encampment," she detailed. "The dog apparently was lying next to what appeared to be a homeless man. We were told later that some people in the area thought he may have been a military veteran."

"Why did they think that?' questioned TJ.

"I think it was the way he was dressed and the conversations that some of the other homeless people had with him."

"And he couldn't care for him?"

"Actually, the homeless man was dead," she explained. "Apparently somebody placed a call to the police to do a welfare check on him."

"That's unfortunate," responded TJ.

"From what I was told, the police tried to check on the man, but the dog growled and would not let them near the lifeless body," she went on. "One of the officers drew his gun and was ready to shoot the dog, thinking that they were going to be attacked. Then the other officer, his partner, said they should call Animal Control, which they did."

"And Animal Control responded?"

"Yes. I'm not sure how Animal Control got the dog away from the man's body, but somehow they were able to take the dog away from the area. And then Animal Control contacted us because they thought they might have to put the dog down. Fortunately, they knew that we were a no kill facility," she said with a smile.

"Well, thank you for your time," said TJ.

"You're welcome."

TJ then turned away and walked out. After getting into his truck, TJ inserted his key into the ignition and was ready to start his truck. But he sat there for a moment. He didn't start his truck.

He wasn't sure why. More than once he placed his fingers on the key. But he did not turn the key to start the truck. After taking a few deep breaths, he got out of his truck and walked back to the building.

As he opened the door and walked into the building, the lady came out of her office with a look of surprise. She just looked at TJ and said, "Hello, again."

"Let me take another look at the Shepherd that you were telling me about," TJ said as he turned toward the aisle. "Do you know what his name is?"

"He had a collar on him with the name Butch," she said.

As the two of them walked down the aisle, the dog, Butch, looked up at them. TJ could see that Butch was looking back at him. No matter where he stepped, Butch did not take his eyes off TJ.

Then TJ looked at the lady and said, "Can you open the cage and let me get close to him?"

"Well, I told you his history," she responded. "He may not be friendly with everyone."

"I know. I'm sure it will be okay."

After the cage was opened, TJ walked in. He got down on one knee to be at eye level with Butch. He then put his hand on top of Butch's head. In a very relaxed manner, Butch raised his head and looked at TJ.

After a few minutes, TJ said, "I'm sure you have some papers for me to complete."

"Yes I do," she responded with a smile.

Within a half hour, Butch and TJ were in the truck, heading down the road.

Chapter Seven

Westward to Kansas

Although his ultimate destination was California, TJ did have to make one more detour before moving on to California. He needed to stop in Kansas to see his friend, and fellow Marine, Tom Harris. Whether in Afghanistan or on leave, Ron Mason, Tom Harris and TJ spent much time together up until Tom completed his service and was discharged.

Tom lived on a farm west of Kansas City, Kansas in a rural area near the town of Lenexa. Tom's father had operated the farm all of his life. The farm had actually been in their family for generations. After Tom was discharged, he was heading back to the farm. Whether he would continue the generational trend was not known—not even to Tom himself. However, from their earlier discussions, the farm was to be his initial destination.

While in Afghanistan, Tom appeared dead set that he would not live out his life as a farmer. But after the continuous dangers he faced during his military service, the farm may have been a respite for him for a while and an opportunity to return to his more serene days. While strongly expressing his aversion to being identified as a farmer, Tom never did talk about any alternative post military career choices. He did not discuss any other plans or desires that he might engage himself in.

As TJ drove west in Missouri heading toward Kansas City, occasionally his thoughts entertained the idea that he could just skip his original plan to stop in Kansas to see Tom. He had gone through the same thoughts previously before seeing Ron's dad and Stacy. He and Ron had made a commitment to see Tom on the way to California. After much deliberation, he eventually came to the conclusion that he would not avoid that commitment. Sometimes just thinking that he had options gave him the feeling that he did have some control of his life.

Driving through areas that he had never seen before gave him a relaxing and comforting feeling. Obviously there were no conversations or discussions. However, he did tend to talk to himself. Being alone and just driving felt good. At times he would glance over at Butch. He could see that Butch appeared relaxed in the back seat of the truck. Maybe he had done this before. Things just seemed right for the two new companions.

When TJ was ready to stop for the night at a motel, he looked to see if pets would be allowed. If nothing was indicated, TJ looked at Butch and said, "Wait here." He did not know if Butch understood the language, or if it was just his tone of voice, but Butch just followed TJ's directions.

If there were no questions about pets at the motel office, then he would just check in. He would then drive to the designated motel unit. After getting out of the truck he would carry in his minimal luggage and check out the motel unit. Next he would go out to lock the truck and have Butch follow him into the unit. Butch would eat whatever was given to him. Of course, TJ knew what not to give him.

The road carried them across Missouri to Kansas City. After crossing the border, they entered Kansas City, Kansas. A short while later, they arrived in Lenexa, Kansas. It was not a large town. The sign indicated a population of about 40,000 people. TJ drove through what he perceived as a main intersection where he saw a coffee shop on the corner of the intersection.

He drove the truck to the back part of the parking lot and allowed Butch to get out and take a short walk to a vacant area, adjacent to the parking lot. When Butch returned, TJ opened the door and let him back in the truck. He then looked up Tom Harris and placed a call to him. The call went to voicemail and TJ left a message for Tom, saying he had arrived in Lenexa. He awaited Tom's return call.

Within a half hour or so, a return call was received. Tom was so excited he could hardly talk. TJ detailed the intersection and the coffee shop where he was parked. Tom said he knew it well. Tom then suggested that he drive over to meet TJ at that intersection. He said that directions to the farm may be confusing, so it would be better to meet TJ at that intersection. He again assured TJ that he knew that location very well. He said he'd be on his way immediately.

Within twenty minutes, Tom drove up in an old pick up truck. When he saw TJ standing by his truck, he drove up next to him and proceeded to get out of his pick up truck. He exhibited some excitement, but appeared to be laboring to get out of his truck. When TJ walked up to him, he could see that Tom had a cast on his left leg that extended beyond his shorts and past his knee.

"TJ," Tom yelled as he gave TJ a hug. "What's it been? About a year?"

"Yes. About a year, if my memory is working correctly," responded TJ.

"You know, when we spent so much time together continuously on a daily basis, on duty or on leave, and then a year goes by, it seems like a lifetime"

"It does," concurred TJ.

TJ couldn't stop looking at the cast on Tom's left leg. "What's that all about?" asked TJ.

"Farm accident. I broke my left leg and damaged something in my left knee helping my dad on the farm," explained Tom.

"You mean you survive three years in Afghanistan and then come back to a pastoral setting on a farm and get injured?" questioned TJ with a grin.

"That's it," responded Tom.

"No trouble driving?" asked TJ

"Boy, that's another story. If it were an automatic transmission, it would be a lot easier. But that old clunker has a clutch. So in addition to healing and toeing with my right foot, I have to use my cane for the clutch, and sometimes for the brake. I think everybody in town must be aware of my driving technique because I see them getting out of the way when they see me coming down the road," Tom explained with a laugh.

"I can understand that," said TJ

"Let's go in the cafe and get a cup of coffee," Tom suggested.

"Okay, sounds good," agreed TJ.

"Oh, you better lock up your truck. Too many thieves in the area, and especially at an intersection like this," suggested Tom.

"No, it'll be alright. My friend will wait here in the truck," said TJ

An inquisitive Tom looked closer, and saw Butch sitting in the passenger seat. Looking back at TJ, he said, "I see. When did you pick up a passenger?"

"It's a long story. Let's get some coffee."

When greeted by the hostess, Tom asked to be seated in a booth. As they sat and waited for their coffees, Tom said, "I knew you would be able to find the farm with my directions, but I wanted to have the opportunity to talk to you privately before you met my parents."

"Okay," said TJ.

"The farm has been in the family forever. My father from his father and his grandfather and beyond," said Tom. "Lately, it's been a little difficult financially. Before I came back home, they almost lost the farm. My father got an emergency loan from a group he saw advertised. He had no choice. It had to be done to avoid a foreclosure."

"So that saved it?" said TJ, following along.

"Kind of," answered Tom. "But the interest is killing him. It's outrageous, but he had no other choice. It was either that or the possibility of losing the farm. I went to these people with my dad to see if we could restructure the loan to make it more reasonable."

"What happened?"

"Well, they wouldn't budge."

"That figures," commented TJ.

"Instead of having him pay wages to a helper on the farm, I have been working with my dad to enable him to save money. I was also working part time at night after working all day on the farm. Then I ended up getting injured," lamented Tom.

"How long are you going to be laid up? Or being somewhat limited in what you can do on the farm?" asked TJ

"It could be another month," responded Tom.

"This might sound crazy to you, because I know nothing about farming, but what if I subbed in for you for a month? Would that help?" inquired TJ.

"That would be a Godsend."

"Well if your parents would agree to provide food and shelter for Butch and myself, then I would agree to help out," offered TJ.

"Butch?"

"My friend in the car," clarified TJ. "We can also share a room," said TJ with a smile.

"Oh, no problem. Believe me, no problem," confirmed Tom.

After they finished their coffee, the two former Marines left the cafe, got in their trucks and TJ followed Tom to the farm.

Chapter Eight

Life on the Farm

As the two trucks entered the farm property, they proceeded to park in an area between the barn and the house. Tom Harris got out of his vehicle and hobbled back to TJ's truck. As he exited his truck, TJ let Butch out to walk around and explore the area.

Tom said, "Come on. I want you to meet my family. Will your dog, I mean your friend, be okay?"

"He'll be fine," assured TJ.

TJ followed Tom as he walked with his cane. He opened the door and TJ followed him into the kitchen. A man and a woman stood before them, smiling.

"Mom, Dad, I want you to meet TJ, my Marine buddy you heard so much about," Tom said as an introduction.

"Hello TJ," his parents responded in unison.

"Hello Mr. and Mrs. Harris," TJ responded. "Pleasure meeting you."

"Guess what? TJ asked if he could stay and help out until I get back on my feet," opened Tom.

TJ just grinned with the news being presented to Tom's parents.

"Well, that's great," said Mrs. Harris.

"Oh, and this is my younger sister, Kathy," said Tom pointing to a young girl sitting in the corner. She did not look up at TJ.

"Hi Kathy. Nice to meet you," said TJ.

Kathy never looked up. TJ figured she was shy, estimating her to be about ten or eleven.

"Let me show you your room," offered Tom.

TJ followed Tom down the hall. In doing so, he passed a small dog in the hallway, giving TJ a feeling of relief, thinking that Butch would also be welcomed as a guest.

Later, as TJ was getting his bags from his truck, Tom said, "I probably should have tipped you off about my sister Kathy."

"A little shy, I guess," TJ offered.

"Actually, she is Autistic," corrected Tom. "She means no disrespect."

"I never took it that way," explained TJ.

"My parents feel awkward about it," furthered Tom. "They've tried everything. They are getting some help from the county."

"Well, I'm glad you told me."

Life on the farm was a total departure from anything TJ had ever experienced before. Although there were farm animals— cows, pigs, chickens, the primary emphasis was on the crops. TJ worked with Tom and his father, literally from sunrise to sunset. Daylight was an important commodity to farmers.

This assembled working contingent would rise at the crack of dawn and start the day with a cup of coffee and maybe a piece of toast. And then it was off to the crop fields and tending to the animals. By mid-morning, there was a gathering at the farmhouse where Tom's mother had a large breakfast for them.

Breakfast was as large a meal as TJ had ever had. And the breakfast was usually consumed by the hungry crew with few leftovers. Then it was back to the chores. At a designated time, they all met back at the farmhouse for lunch. This was their lightest meal. Soon after, they were back to their chores. Much had to be done while the sun was cooperating with them.

As darkness descended on the farm, the group of three would climax their activities and complete the work of the day. Then it was back to the farmhouse where a large meal was prepared by Tom's mother for dinner. Had the proposed menu of the day been presented to TJ a day before, he would have declined the extent of the meals that were to be served. However, during any day of the routine, the working crew had no problem consuming the food that was served for any of the meals.

Following the dinner meal, they all engaged in various activities—reading newspapers, watching television, or just being engaged in various conversations. At an early hour, they all retired to their bedrooms for the evening. TJ, like the others, seemed to have no problem going to sleep. Sunrise would be on its way. It was this part of the activities that reminded him of his days in boot camp.

Butch slept in the bedroom with TJ. Frequently, before going to bed, TJ would take Butch for a ride in his truck. They would stop a short distance from the farm where Butch was able to have a run with TJ. It was a continuation of the bonding between the two of them

The farm life seemed to have a calming affect on TJ. He had never lived on, or visited, a farm before. But the experience was comforting to him. He thought that maybe the absence of turmoil and confrontation that he had experienced in the past was a contributing factor to his comfort and well being.

Each day blended into the next one. Tom, because of his injury, was not able to be an equal partner with TJ in completing the chores. But he did what he could and was a complement to the efforts of TJ and Tom's father. The required activities were being completed by the three.

On one particular day, Tom's mother had gone to the market to replenish the shelves with food for the large volume of meals that she prepared. As always, she was accompanied by her daughter, Kathy. Apparently, she took the truck with the stick shift, and drove to the market and other stores in town. After the purchased provisions were loaded onto the truck, she drove home. At home she unloaded the truck and stocked the shelves, refrigerator and freezer.

One day, realizing how much was being purchased on her shopping trip, TJ commented, "You did that all by yourself?"

Tom's mother just looked at him, smiled and said, "If not me, then who?"

TJ just smiled back at her.

On that particular day, Tom's mother said, "Oh, by the way, I was able to get some special dog treats for Butch. I realize that he seems content with the food that you have been feeding him as well as the scraps that are given to him from the meals, but we're all entitled to some treats in life on occasion."

TJ smiled and responded with, "Thank you. That was very kind of you." It really did give TJ a warm feeling knowing that he, along with Butch, were accepted by Tom's family.

Butch appeared to be content with the lifestyle on the farm. He had room to roam, was properly fed, and just waited each day at the farmhouse for TJ to return from his farm chores. Later the two of them would take a ride in the truck to various destinations in the area. The truck rides also enabled TJ to explore the area and there were many opportunities for Butch to run.

Tom's mother continued her discussion with TJ. "Butch seems to be a very intelligent dog. I've been around animals, and in particular dogs, all my life. He always seems to be aware of what's happening. What breed is he?"

"Well, I got him from an animal rescue group. They told me that he was a Shepherd. Apparently, as I was told, the breed goes back to 2000 B.C. They were used to watch over and guide livestock in Turkey."

During the conversation, Butch just sat there listening.

"That's interesting," she responded. "You say it's a Shepherd. I wonder what kind of Shepherd."

"Actually, they told me it was an Anatolian Shepherd. I had never heard of that breed before," answered TJ.

"He just seems to be very adaptable," she further commented. "Oh, here we are talking and I'm guessing that Butch acknowledged that he heard me say that I got some special dog treats today."

While Butch was sitting near them, Kathy had come into the kitchen earlier and began to pet Butch. She put her hand on his head and then began to pet him on his back. By his reaction, it seemed very comforting to Butch.

Then Tom's mother said, "Kathy, would you like to give Butch some of those dog treats that we brought home from the store."

Kathy responded by walking over to the counter and opening up the bag of treats. She took the bag and walked over to Butch. Saying nothing, she fumbled with the treats in the bag. She finally took some out and, with an open hand, held them out for Butch. He gently ate the treats from her hand. This brought a smile to her. She then proceeded the routine and continued to reward Butch.

Tom's mother and TJ smiled as they watched the activity unfold.

"He seems to understand her and is patient with her," Tom's mother observed.

"Each day I learn more about him," observed TJ.

It was one of those moments that each of them would always remember—Kathy and Butch, both accepting each other.

One day, after Tom and TJ completed their daily work in the fields and their dinner meal had ended, the two of them were relaxing in chairs on the front porch. Tom said, "Let's take a ride to town and get a beer."

"Sounds good," responded TJ.

It didn't take long before the two of them were in TJ's truck and headed to town. Butch was riding in the rear seat of the truck. TJ felt that this was a good way to end a full day of work.

Then Tom opened with, "By the way, I wanted to ask you something. Actually, I have an offer for you."

"Okay," responded TJ, smiling because he knew Tom so well.

"You see, my mother got us involved in something," explained Tom

"Us?"

"Well, kind of," said Tom. "You see, a friend of my mother got word from an acquaintance of hers that one of the teachers at the junior high school, as part of her course curriculum, wanted to bring in a military veteran to speak to her class."

"And?" said TJ, following along.

"Well, knowing my mother, she volunteered me to speak to the class before she ever discussed it with me. I mean, I'm committed to this," explained Tom.

"How does this involve me?" responded TJ with half a smirk.

"Oh, come on. I can't do this myself. I get tongue tied and sometimes I forget what I want to say," offered Tom. "We could go as a team, the two of us. It would be great."

"You're serious. You really feel that you need me there?" asked TJ, knowing what the response would be.

"Yep. It will be great for the two of us," assured Tom.

"I don't know," responded TJ. "I have some reservations about those types of situations."

"Why?" questioned Tom.

"Since I've been back, I've run across so many people that found out that I was in Afghanistan. They always say the usual thank you for your service," said TJ. "You can see it in their face, or hear it in their voice that they're saying what they read or were told to say to a returning veteran. They have no idea what it was like. But they feel that they're supposed to say something like that."

"I know what you're saying. I see it too," concurred Tom.

"It's like they check it off their list. Telling themselves that they did the right thing. They think that it's the proper thing to say to someone in the service," TJ went on. "Thank you for your service."

"Sometimes it is meaningful from some of them," added Tom. "To others, I guess it's just being politically correct."

"I'm sure it's something that started with the banks. Since they try to gouge you all the time with their numerous and exorbitant fees, they think they can do an offset by conveying an insincere expression to you. I guess that way they consider themselves to be caring people by telling you to have a nice day. Some even go beyond that and tell you to have a fantastic day. Call it what it is. It's all bullshit," TJ concluded.

"I'm not disagreeing with you. But will you help me out here. You know I never volunteered for it," Tom further explained.

"Okay, we'll do it," agreed TJ.

"Great. I told them to tell the teacher that we can meet with her tomorrow night for coffee and discuss the presentation," said Tom.

"You already committed me to this?" questioned TJ. Realistically, TJ was not that surprised by Tom's approach. He knew Tom.

"You'll enjoy it," said Tom. "After all, what are buddies for?"

Chapter Nine

Teacher's Meeting

On the designated day to meet with the school teacher, Tom and TJ reduced their work schedule to make it a shorter day of work on the farm. They came back to the farmhouse, had a light dinner and took showers in preparation for their meeting. TJ drove the two of them to the designated meeting place, a familiar coffee shop in town. As Tom had informed TJ, he had never met the teacher, but had only spoken to her by telephone. He apparently told her to look for two guys sitting in one of the booths in the back of the coffee shop at around seven thirty in the evening.

The two of them sat in the booth on the same side of the table, facing the front entrance. They both would look up as various patrons continued to open the door and enter. Eventually, they observed a lady, ranging in age from sixty to seventy, walk in and start to look around.

"This might be her," said Tom as he began to rise from his seat.

Just then, the lady waived to someone on the other side of the coffee shop, and started to walk toward a table where two other women were seated.

"I guess not," said Tom, with his usual sly grin.

TJ responded with a grin of his own.

Ten minutes later, in walked an attractive lady, mid to late twenties. She had light brown hair that didn't quite reach her shoulders. As she looked around, she spotted the two men sitting in the booth in the back of the coffee shop, and began walking toward them. Before she got to the booth, the two men began to rise from their seats to greet her.

"Ms. Adams?" opened Tom.

"Yes," she responded.

"Ms. Adams, hello, I'm Tom Harris and this is my friend, TJ Ward," as he presented themselves to her

"Hello, I'm Sandra Adams," she responded. "It's nice to meet the two of you. But since we're not in the classroom, you can just call me Sandy."

"As you probably know from my mother, we've both been discharged from the United States Marines," said Tom.

"I did know that. Actually, your mother told that to a common friend of ours, who passed it on to me. She became aware of the fact that I was trying to get someone to talk to my students who had actual experience in military service," Sandy explained.

"Well we can certainly fit that bill," responded Tom. "Do you think some of your students might be interested in joining the military?" asked Tom.

"I really don't know," answered Sandy. "But I probably should completely explain my motivation for this effort."

Tom and TJ leaned forward in their seats, eager to listen to her as she began her explanation.

"Not long ago, I attended a conference for teachers," she began. "It included various concurrent sessions in which we were able to select any of the sessions offered that might be of interest to us. What I thought would be interesting and intriguing was one with a panel that included Ken Burns as one of the speakers. As you know, Ken Burns is the documentary film maker. He did such productions as *The Civil War, Jackie Robinson, Jazz* and several others."

"That sounds like it would have been interesting," said TJ.

"Yes it was. During that discussion, Ken Burns brought up his involvement in the production and the making of *The Civil War.*

He stated that after completing that work, he felt that he could not make another war documentary," she continued. "Going through the wartime letters, speeches, and documents were so emotionally draining that he did not want to go through any similar exercises."

"I can understand that," said Tom.

"But, as we know, he later made a great documentary about World War II called *The War*," Sandy went on. "He explained that he saw a survey taken among high school students that was difficult to understand. The survey stated that over fifty per cent of the students thought that the United States and Germany had joined forces to fight Russia in World War II. He said that after he heard that, he was prompted and inspired to produce *The War*.

Tom and TJ continued to listen to Sandy. TJ became very captivated by Sandy as he listened to her express her feelings. She seemed like the kind of person that one could sit and listen to for hours as she spoke—probably about almost anything.

"After listening to Ken Burns talk about his effort to educate more people about our history, I just felt very motivated to do whatever I could. And there I was—a teacher who wanted to take on that mission. I certainly have that opportunity to advance that cause. And I guess that's where you fellows come into the picture," she summarized.

"Well said," responded TJ. "We're willing to do our part."

Tom nodded in agreement.

The three of them then discussed arrangements and details regarding the presentation by Tom and TJ to Sandy's class at the junior high school. Before they departed, the three of them exchanged cell phone numbers.

As Tom and TJ drove back to the farm, TJ was thinking about how persuasive Sandy was in her efforts. She had a purpose and she certainly was able to get them to go along with her plan. They were looking forward to giving a presentation.

"She's quite a lady," TJ commented to Tom.

"You got that right, TJ," Tom agreed.

Chapter Ten

Class Presentation

During the next few days, TJ could not get Sandy out of his mind. He could not recall when he had ever met someone that he felt he could spend a lot of time with. She was also a very nice looking lady with an attractive smile. At times he would kid himself by thinking that he wouldn't mind being back in school again.

On the scheduled day of their presentation, Tom and TJ ended their farm chores at noon. They showered and dressed for the occasion. They were both looking forward to the presentation at the school. It was also an opportunity for TJ to see Sandy again. Instead of just thinking about her, he would actually be able to be with her in person.

The two designated guests went in and waited for Sandy in the school administration office. A short time later, Sandy arrived in the office smiling, as TJ had been visualizing. She greeted them and led them to her classroom. The two of them stood behind Sandy's desk in the front of the room. After the students settled in their seats, Sandy addressed the class.

"As I have been promising, we have a special treat today," she began. "We have an opportunity to hear from two former members of the United States Marine Corps that are here with us today. I'd like you to meet Tom Harris and TJ Ward."

A short applause from the class greeted the two veterans. As they sat in the designated seats in the front of the classroom, Tom began the presentation.

"Hello, I'm Tom Harris and this is TJ Ward. We are honored to be here to discuss our part in the service to our country and to answer any questions that you might have. And, by the way I should mention that we are not on a recruiting mission for the Marines or for any other branch of the service."

The latter explanation was met with some laughter.

"As many of you may realize, the draft is not in operation at this time," Tom explained. "However, when the draft was in operation, nobody was drafted into the Marines. It has been a volunteer branch of the service and continues to remain so."

The students seemed to be settling in and listening to Tom as he spoke to them.

"The two of us joined the Marines, went through boot camp in North Carolina and eventually served in Afghanistan. We felt that it was an honor to serve in the Marines and to serve our country. However, I'll be honest with you. While we were in boot camp and going through some difficult training exercises, many times we would individually say to ourselves—'what am I doing here and what was I thinking about when I got into this?' You see, in boot camp, they break you down as an individual. Their objective was to make you become part of a unit. When somebody screws up in the unit, the unit is punished. Additional work details and extended exercises will follow."

He paused for a moment and took a drink from his water bottle.

"Let me give you an analogy. It would be like a father of three boys coming home after work and finding that his fishing gear and equipment was damaged. He's mad. Instead of asking questions to determine who the culprit was, he decides to spank all three sons. Is it right? No, but we're not looking at right or wrong. A bonded unit is being developed."

Tom paused and realized he had a very attentive group.

"You cease thinking as an individual. Instead, you became part of a unit. Part of the team. That's how you're molded. You don't want the people in your unit to be punished for something you did. Instead of thinking what you are going through, you think more about what your unit is going through. A brotherhood evolves. You become bonded with each other in the unit. You think as a unit, if that makes any sense.

Again, Tom paused to take a drink.

"In boot camp, I can recall our drill sergeant telling us that when we hear the Marine Marching song, we will stand proudly. To a person, we were thinking that this guy is crazy. Who the heck is he trying to kid? As a group, we all felt that he was so wrong. But you know, eventually, as time went on, and to this day, we feel proud when we hear it played. We realized later that he was right. He knew us better than we knew ourselves at that time."

The students continued to be very attentive and seemed eager to listen as Tom spoke to them. Sandy sat to the side listening to the discussion and observing her students. Tom continued, and eventually completed his part of the presentation.

"And now I would like to have TJ speak to you about his thoughts and impressions about our service with the Marines," expressed Tom. "TJ, you now have the honors."

TJ leaned forward in his seat, looked at the students and began, "I certainly concur with Tom about our feelings in boot camp and how we felt as new volunteers in The United States Marine Corps. But I am going to be very objective and honest with this class because you deserve nothing less than that."

As he stood up, he had the attention of the class.

"I don't know how many of you have seen or recall the movie *Top Gun* with Tom Cruise. Well, in that movie, the character played by Tom Cruise, was a pilot. He lost his best friend, also a pilot, in an aerial attack. During a later scene in the movie, Tom Cruise was engaged in an aerial dogfight with enemy planes. During that scene he started to take a few moments to think about his good friend who died as a result of being shot down by an enemy plane. At that point, he became determined to retaliate and shoot down the enemy pilot. He was successful. He avenged the personal loss of his friend."

The response from the students ranged from smiles to complete attention.

"Well, that was Hollywood—the movies. Realistically, it doesn't happen that way. You're trained, from boot camp forward, to react to situations. You don't think and analyze situations when you are in combat. You just react. That's what you were trained to do. To a combat veteran, a scene like that in the movie is just bullshit."

Not a sound was heard from anyone in the classroom.

"Your motivation in battle is to stay alive and to do whatever you can to keep your combat buddy alive. When you lose a buddy, you usually don't have time to grieve. You just move on. You have to. It's war. You react. You don't take the time to think and analyze a situation."

TJ paused for a moment, and then went on.

"Sometimes you return to your quarters and know that the bunk near yours is going to be empty. That's because the occupant is never going to return. You can't help but notice the pictures—it could be a wife, a child or a girlfriend, and you also see an article of clothing that will not be worn again. You leave to go to the mess hall. Upon your return, all the personal gear and the pictures are gone. There is no time to grieve the loss. The space is taken by another occupant. It's that type of life that you're living. It's nothing like you ever experienced before. But you're in a war time situation."

The classroom was a captive audience.

"Sometimes you think back to when you were at home. There were times when people became angry about events that they felt affected them. Waiting in line for a movie, getting irritated about a price increase, or not being able to get what they want. These things created anger in many people. In combat, thinking about things that make people angry at home can be a source of anger for a soldier. But I want to tell you that anger is not such a bad thing when you are in combat. You need to be angry. You're facing an enemy. It's kill or be killed, whether that applies to you or your combat buddy. You need to be angry and hate your opposition."

TJ paused for a moment and took a drink from the water bottle he brought with him.

"As I said," he went on, "Anger is necessary in combat. If you took the time to think about everything, you would realize that the enemy that you're fighting may be doing it for patriotic or religious reasons. You may start thinking that their motivation is understandable. After all, they're human. But you can't allow yourself to think that way. Again, your objectives are to stay alive and protect your combat buddy."

Once again, TJ paused and took a drink from his bottle.

"In our country, I often hear about efforts to get people to vote. The ads state that our armed forces fought for that right. In combat, that's probably the furthest thing from our minds. We don't really give a shit if someone votes or if they don't vote. I know I'm repeating myself, but in combat, it's staying alive and protecting your buddy. Thank you for your attention."

Sandy arose from her chair and said, "We'd like to thank our guests for their presentation."

The students responded with an applause for their guest speakers.

"With only a few minutes remaining, we'll end today's class at this time," Sandy instructed her class. She then led her guests down the hall and to the front door of the school.

"Thank you gentlemen," she said. "I need to take care of something at this time. She walked away from them and down the hall.

Tom and TJ left the building and walked to the truck.

As they drove off in the truck, TJ said, "That really ended abruptly."

"I looked at her face as you were talking and I think she was not completely in tune with some of your language," explained Tom.

"Really?" expressed TJ, somewhat surprised. "I thought she wanted realism. You know, not something sugarcoated."

"Well, that's the way I was reading her," said Tom.

Chapter Eleven

Contact with Sandy

TJ had not heard from Sandy after the presentation to her class. Not that there was any mention that she would contact him or Tom, but in his mind he anticipated that they had something in common. Maybe that was just how he saw it.

He decided to call her. Waiting until the time that her class would have ended, he placed a call to her cell phone. It went to voicemail. As he listened to the voicemail message, he admitted to himself that he liked hearing her voice again.

At the prompt, he said, "Hi Sandy. It's TJ. When you have a minute, could you give me a call?" Then he left his cell phone number.

No return call was received. He waited that night, and still no call was forthcoming. Well, she was probably busy—maybe with parents, grading papers or whatever teachers do when they don't have the students in front of them he rationalized.

He went to sleep that night making excuses to himself as to why she hadn't returned his call.

The next day he and Tom continued to do their farm work. Periodically, he would check his cell phone. Still, no return call. He decided to put it out of his mind, telling himself that she was in class and probably didn't have the opportunity to call him. Or maybe she thought she should not bother him while he was doing his work at the farm. As he and Tom completed their work for the day, they headed to the farmhouse for the evening meal.

TJ decided to place another call to Sandy's cell phone. He had not mentioned anything to Tom about trying to contact Sandy. That night he and Butch followed their normal routine with a ride in the truck to an out of the way area. This would give him the privacy he needed. He dialed Sandy's cell phone number. His attempt again went to voicemail. "Hi Sandy, it's TJ again. I'm sure you're pretty busy, but I wanted to see if you had a few minutes to talk." Again, he left his cell phone number.

The next night, after the evening meal was served, TJ excused himself, went to his room, and checked to see if he received a return call. His cell phone showed no incoming call. He was starting to feel a little frustrated and irritated. A few hours later, when he had some privacy, he tried to place another call. The result was the same—voicemail. He just hung up without leaving a message.

He started thinking about this situation. Maybe Tom was right. Was she really upset with him about the manner in which he made his presentation to her students? TJ could not imagine that he would not see her again. He was starting to think that she desired to have nothing to do with him. But then he thought she didn't seem to be that kind of person. The cell phone wasn't going to work. He would have to see her in person.

The next day, TJ told Tom and his dad that he had to take care of some business in town. He let them know that he would not be there for dinner. He left the fields early and came back to the farmhouse to shower and change clothes. Before he left, he looked back at Butch and said he'd be back later. It was customary for him to talk to Butch that way. When he first would say something to Butch, he didn't know if Butch would understand him. After a few occasions, it seemed that Butch understood him. So this was one of those times when TJ left in his truck without Butch. He knew Butch would be fine that night.

TJ drove to the school and entered what appeared to be the faculty parking area. He strategically positioned his truck to allow himself a vantage point to see when the faculty members would be leaving the building. He waited for what seemed to be an extended period, but realistically, it was probably a half hour.

Eventually people were beginning to leave the building. And then finally he saw Sandy emerge from the door with another lady. They stopped and had a conversation for a few minutes. Then the other lady walked over to a car while Sandy walked in a different direction. TJ got out of his truck and slowly walked toward Sandy as she approached a small compact car.

TJ walked toward her. When he was about ten or twelve feet from her, he said "Sandy. Hi, it's TJ."

"Oh hello," she responded. "What brings you here?"

"I tried to call you," he answered. "I needed to talk to you."

"I'm sorry. I meant to call you. I've just been very busy," she tried to explain.

"I have the impression that you're not too happy with me," TJ offered. "I would just like a few minutes of your time to explain. And if necessary, to apologize."

"That won't be necessary," she answered.

"Please. If I can just be heard," he pressed.

"Okay," she agreed.

"I noticed a coffee shop a block or so away. Let me buy you a cup of coffee. Or tea or a coke. My treat," as he was trying to persuade her with a little humor.

"Okay. Let me follow you," she said.

"My truck is right over there. I'll meet you there."

TJ got into his truck and drove to the coffee shop. During half of the drive he was constantly checking his rear view mirror, hoping that Sandy would not change her mind. She didn't. They each drove to the coffee shop and parked in the adjoining parking lot.

TJ got out of his truck and walked over to Sandy's car. After she emerged from her vehicle, they walked to the entrance of the coffee shop. Few people were present during that late afternoon. The two of them were led to a booth. They seated themselves across from each other.

As they sat together, TJ opened with, "Sandy, I'm sorry if I came on a little strong in my presentation to your class. I didn't mean to offend anyone, especially you. That was the last thing I wanted to do."

Sandy smiled and responded, "I don't feel that I was offended. I'm not even sure if anyone in the class was offended. At least nobody approached me to tell me that they were offended"

"Well that makes me feel better," responded TJ

"Believe it or not, my concern was really focused on some of the parents," she said. "So far, no parent has called me. And I haven't heard anything from the principal, assuming that maybe some parents may have called him. So far, nothing."

"Well that's good," said TJ, feeling somewhat better.

"The more I thought about it, the more I realized that I did want to expose my students to the events of the real world," Sandy explained. "And you certainly presented the situation from the perspective of a combat veteran."

TJ responded with a smile. "I like your perspective and I like your approach to teaching. When we first met, that impressed me."

"Thank you. I appreciate that."

"As I sat and listened to you when we first met, I found myself being drawn to you, listening to everything you were saying," expressed TJ. "I didn't want you to stop explaining anything to us. You have a way with words."

"Don't embarrass me. I'm just trying to do a good job of teaching," responded Sandy.

"Sorry. I don't want to make you feel uncomfortable," explained TJ.

"I know you don't mean to do that," said Sandy. "I really have to get going."

"Okay. Would you let me take you to dinner? Tomorrow, or the day after, or whenever your schedule would allow me to do that. It would mean a lot to me," pursued TJ.

"Let's do that tomorrow," Sandy responded.

"Great. I'll pick you up at six, or seven. What would be best?" TJ offered.

"Let's make it six thirty," said Sandy.

"It's a deal," assured TJ. And Sandy gave TJ her address.

The next day TJ arrived in the area of Sandy's apartment at quarter after six. Careful not to arrive too early, he just waited in his truck two blocks away. He was really looking forward to spending time with Sandy. It would be nice, he thought, if she might be feeling the same. At the same time, he was hoping that she was not simply following through with an obligation or commitment to have dinner with him.

At six thirty TJ knocked on the door of Sandy's apartment. She answered the door and invited TJ into her apartment. She lived there alone. It appeared to be a one bedroom apartment with a small kitchen and a dining area. TJ couldn't help but notice the table in the dining area filled with books and papers from school.

As Sandy observed TJ looking at the table, she said to him, "That's my working area. There's a small portion of the table where I eat my meals, but the rest of the table pretty much serves as my desk at home."

TJ smiled and said, "Whatever works and whatever is comfortable."

Within a few minutes the two of them were ready to go to dinner. Having conferred with Tom's family, TJ became aware of a nice restaurant to take Sandy to dinner. As they drove into the parking area, Sandy looked at TJ and said, "We really don't need anything fancy. I'm pretty much a down to earth person."

"I just thought this would be a nice restaurant for a dinner. It's probably not a place where I would frequent that often. In fact I have never been here, but I was told it was a good restaurant," TJ explained.

The two of them were rewarded with a nice dinner. The service was very good. The venue was quiet enough to enable them to have a conversation without fighting any noisy televisions or loud music. The background music was very accommodating for an intimate dinner.

They talked about their backgrounds and what brought them to the area. Sandy grew up in rural Kansas. She attended and graduated from Washburn University in Topeka, Kansas. The school was affordable and had less than seven thousand undergraduates, which she felt was a good fit for her. She said it seemed right for her, as opposed to the University of Kansas or Kansas State University. Those schools and their campuses had too much of a big city atmosphere for her. From the beginning of college, she was intent on becoming a teacher.

TJ talked to Sandy about growing up in the suburban Chicago area in Brookfield. He mentioned that he and his close friend, Ron Mason, were friends in high school and the two of them were in college together. He further explained that they both joined the Marines. Together, after boot camp, they served in Afghanistan.

Sandy was a good listener. She seemed very interested as TJ talked about his upbringing and his earlier years. As a student of history, she had an interest in peoples' lives. After TJ laid out his background, Sandy looked at him and asked, "Well then, what brought you to Kansas?"

TJ looked down for a moment, showing some emotion and said. "Well, it might seem crazy, but I wasn't intending to be in Kansas. It was just a quick stop on the way to California."

"That's interesting," said Sandy, appearing to be waiting to hear the story. "Why California?"

"My friend Ron had been to California with his parents when he was younger, and loved it," TJ explained. "We had a plan to go to California following our discharges from the Marines and our return from Afghanistan."

"And plans changed?"

"Yes. Unfortunately, we lost Ron in Afghanistan."

"Oh, I'm sorry," expressed Sandy.

"It may seem crazy, but I decided to follow through with the plans that Ron and I had in getting to California," explained TJ.

"I don't think anything is crazy," assured Sandy.

TJ was speaking very softly and slowly. "My stop in Kansas was to see one of our Marine buddies. That was Tom, who you have already met. Unfortunately, he had a farm injury and wasn't able to assist his father, especially during the planting season. So I offered to stay on to help out at the farm. In a sense I would sub for Tom until he was on his feet, so to speak."

"Well, there are some good results with you staying for a while," said Sandy.

"You mean helping at the farm?" asked TJ.

"Yes, that's true. And also, we wouldn't be having this dinner if you made Kansas a whistle stop."

"That's also true," said TJ with a smile.

"I probably should get going," said Sandy. "I enjoyed the time that we spent together. I'm sorry I was so inquisitive and caused you to be uncomfortable about the situation with your friend."

"Don't be sorry. It's just something I have to deal with."

Sandy and TJ left the restaurant, not realizing that they had been there for over two hours. TJ drove to Sandy's apartment and got out of the truck to walk her to the door.

"I really enjoyed having dinner with you," Sandy said.

"I very much enjoyed being with you, as I have since Tom and I first met you at the coffee shop," responded TJ.

The two of them looked into each other's eyes for a moment. TJ then reached out to Sandy's hand and gently held it.

"Good night," he said as he turned to leave.

"Call me," said Sandy before she quietly closed the door

Chapter Twelve

Time With Sandy

On the way back to the farm and for the rest of the evening, TJ kept hearing the last words that Sandy had said to him that night—"Call me." It was very pleasing to him. He liked her from the start when he and Tom first met her at the coffee shop to discuss their presentation. Later, for a while, he harbored fears that he may never have the opportunity to see her or be with her again. He was now over that hurdle.

He knows he fought very hard to reconnect with her with his phone calls and then eventually meeting her in the school parking lot. He wanted so badly to give Sandy an opportunity to know the real TJ. In their discussion of so many different topics during their dinner, TJ felt that she had become more comfortable with him.

After he had driven her home and walked her to her door, TJ was feeling that they were developing a good relationship. As he looked into her eyes and she responded by looking back into his eyes, the feeling was good. At the same time he didn't want to come on too strong or give Sandy the impression that he was being somewhat aggressive. That's why he reached out and gently and softly held her hand.

When she responded with, "Call me," her words made him feel that he did the right thing at the right time. He knew that he would definitely follow through and call her.

The next night TJ was getting ready to call Sandy. He started to think that maybe he should wait a day or two. But no, he decided to call her that night.

TJ dialed Sandy's number. After two rings, she answered, "Hello."

"Hello Sandy, it's TJ. How are you?"

"Just fine. Just relaxing, and looking over my class plans for the next day," she explained.

"Oh, I won't take up much of your time. I just wanted to tell you that I really enjoyed our dinner last night."

"I enjoyed it very much myself," she responded. "We never seemed to run out of things to talk about."

"I was very comfortable and felt very relaxed while sharing so many thoughts with you," TJ said. "I was going to ask you if you had any plans for this Saturday."

"No, nothing special," she responded. "What did you have in mind?"

"I thought that maybe I could pick you up and we could take a ride around the area. There's so much that I have not had an opportunity to see," he offered.

"There is a local museum in town. We could start there. After that, we can just see what would be of interest to us," Sandy presented. "How does ten on Saturday morning sound to you?'

"Sounds great. I'll see you at your place on Saturday at ten. Good night. See you Saturday," TJ concluded.

"Good night, TJ."

As he concluded the call, he was all smiles.

On Saturday morning, TJ arrived at the door of Sandy's apartment at exactly ten o'clock. They left and Sandy directed him to the museum, as they had discussed. Realistically for TJ, it could have been a museum, a hardware store, or any other place. He just found himself enjoying the company of Sandy. She made him feel comfortable when he was with her. He was also feeling good about himself—better than he had in a long time.

After the museum, feeling hungry, Sandy suggested that they stop at a drive through hot dog stand. They sat and ate in the truck.

TJ was thinking that there were only about six weeks before the school year would conclude. He was curious about her plans that summer.

"Not too long before this school year ends," he opened.

"No, it won't be very long," Sandy responded. "As is the routine, I received my usual pink slip from the school administration."

"Really," responded TJ. "You mean you won't be teaching at the school any longer?"

"Well, not necessarily," said Sandy. "As I indicated, it's a routine for the school administrators. This is done with all the teachers. So as not to show any discrimination toward any particular teachers, they send them out to all the teachers."

"I wasn't aware of that," said TJ

"That way they're not violating any provisions of the budget for the next school year. They're guaranteed not to exceed the budget limits that way. Then about four to six weeks before the new school year is ready to begin, they send out the hiring contracts," she explained.

"What most of us teachers do is apply for unemployment benefits during the summer months. After all, in effect, we have a termination notice in hand by having the pink slip. That enables us to collect unemployment benefits," she further explained.

Sandy and TJ began seeing each other more frequently during the next few weeks. They had gone to the movie theater, out to dinner, and just for some rides through the countryside. On one particular Friday night, after TJ had taken Sandy out to dinner, he drove her back to her apartment. After she asked, he confirmed that he did not have to be up early the next morning. She then invited him in for a cup of coffee.

A short time later, Sandy looked at TJ and said, "I've enjoyed our time together. In fact I have for all these weeks that we have been seeing each other. Maybe tonight you won't have to leave here with just a handshake."

TJ responded with a smile that he could not hold back. No other words needed to be spoken between them. Looking into each others' eyes expressed their desires.

Chapter Thirteen

Sandy's Concerns

Sandy and TJ continued to see each other whenever an opportunity presented itself. Sometimes they would just go to a park or take a long drive in the area. Usually on drives in the area, they were accompanied by Butch, who sat in the back seat of the truck.

On one occasion, while Sandy and TJ walked in the park with Butch, they stopped at one of the park benches to take a brief rest. As they sat on the bench and enjoyed the scenery, Sandy looked at TJ and told him that there was something that concerned her. She told him that she enjoyed being together with him, but at times he seemed very distant. She thought he might be thinking of the past, and possibly about his friend, Ron Mason. Other times she thought he might be dwelling on unpleasant memories of his upbringing. Occasionally she thought his mood seemed to change and he appeared to be harboring some anger.

As TJ listened to Sandy, he responded by saying that, yes he agreed, there were times when he would be thinking about the past events in his life. Sometimes they were hard to shake.

Sandy said she could understand that. But what she suggested is that it might be a good idea for him to see a professional. She felt that it might help him to deal with the situations that he has gone through in his life. She explained that it was important for him as well as for the two of them at this time and for their future.

Although feeling somewhat reluctant, TJ agreed to take that step. Initially, it may have been an accommodation to Sandy. Although he did not see the benefit, he could see how serious it was to her. He felt very strong about not wanting to displease her.

Working with Sandy, the two of them researched the names and backgrounds of various professional psychologists. They were able to find one who had a background in working with military veterans—Dr. Mark Howard. He had actually been in the military himself. An appointment was set for TJ to see Dr. Howard.

After TJ had arrived at the office of Dr. Mark Howard, he was given some paperwork to be completed before he would meet with Dr. Howard. After completing the paperwork, as best as he could, he presented it to the assistant sitting at the desk in the lobby. She thanked him and asked him to take a seat. "Dr. Howard will be with you shortly," she said.

Within a few minutes, the inner office door opened and a tall, slender man came out of the office. He smiled at TJ and said, "Hello Mr. Ward, I'm Mark Howard. He held out his hand to greet TJ. "Please come in."

TJ followed Dr. Howard into the office.

"Please have a seat," said Dr. Howard as he gestured toward two seats that were set approximately four to five feet apart from each other.

As TJ sat down in one of the seats, Dr. Howard sat down in the other.

"I didn't know if there would be a couch for me to lie down on while you sat in the chair and asked me questions," TJ opened the conversation.

"No," Dr. Howard responded with a smile. "I don't know if anyone uses a couch anymore. Maybe in the movies. Anyway, I don't use a couch."

TJ just nodded to that response.

"Let me take a minute and glance over your paperwork," he began. "Do you go by Terry?"

"Only to my family and my teachers," he responded. "All my friends identify me as TJ."

"Okay, then TJ it is. I'm Mark Howard, and I'm just as comfortable when people call me Mark," he explained, "Unless, of course, when I make a call to get a dinner reservation. In that case, I always identify myself as Dr. Howard."

"I'll probably just stay with Dr. Howard," said TJ.

"Whatever you're comfortable with is fine with me."

TJ smiled in response.

"It says that you have been told that you have some anger issues," opened Dr. Howard.

"Yes,"

"Do you feel that you, yourself, have some anger issues?" questioned Dr. Howard.

"Well, maybe. Under the certain circumstances or in some situations, there might be some anger," responded TJ.

TJ then talked about his family and the earlier years. And then he talked about Ron Mason—explaining that they grew up together, went to college together and eventually went into the Marines together. Then TJ became emotional when he talked about the loss of Ron Mason in combat.

"Realistically, it should have been me instead of Ron who was killed in battle. If it wasn't for the incident with my ammunition belt, then it would have been me," TJ explained.

"I can see that it is weighing heavily on you," commented Dr. Howard.

"Yes, of course. Why wouldn't it"

"I agree. And realistically I would add that these circumstances would be difficult for anyone to deal with. To be troubled by what you went through is a normal reaction," commented Dr. Howard.

TJ did not expect that kind of response.

"Before I was discharged, I had gone through some sessions with some of the military psychologists and psychiatrists. They listened, but said very little. Then they prescribed some drugs," TJ explained. "I had no further interest in talking to any more shrinks. To be honest with you, I was somewhat reluctant to come here."

"Well, let me try to put your mind somewhat at ease. I am a psychologist. I cannot prescribe drugs for you. If I thought that drugs would be the remedy, I would have to refer you to a psychiatrist, or as you say, to a shrink," Dr. Howard went on. "A psychiatrist is also a medical doctor. That is why they can prescribe drugs to a patient. At this time I have no intention for such a referral."

"Okay. I understand."

"As you explained, you and Ron Mason went through high school and college together. That's a long time. And then the two of you joined the United States Marines, and served in combat in Afghanistan. It's completely understandable that a lifelong friendship existed."

"Yes," responded TJ

"I'm getting to know you today. I didn't know Ron Mason. But maybe, through you, I can learn something about Ron. Tell me something about Ron that stands out in your mind. It could be a story, or some incident that you may have recalled," Dr. Howard requested.

"I can tell about a story, well an incident, that I observed that taught me something about life that I will never forget," TJ responded. "Ron was an only child. Since he would be going to college after he graduated from high school, his parents bought him a new car."

"That's a nice graduation gift," commented Dr. Howard.

"Yes. It was great. When he and I were at college, that was our transportation," said TJ. "One day he brought it to the dealer for an oil change and the required maintenance. At that time, we were hearing a definite rattling coming from the engine compartment.

We didn't know what it was. He told the service advisor at the dealership about it. When Ron picked up his car and came back to the campus, the rattle was still there."

"No service regarding the rattle?" questioned Dr. Howard.

"No," answered TJ. "Ron brought the car back a week later, told them about the rattle and left it with the dealership. When he picked up his car, the rattle was still there. It became a constant source of annoyance."

"I'm assuming that he didn't ask his father to take care of the problem," Dr. Howard presumed.

"Not a chance, not Ron. I was with Ron a week later when he took his car back and confronted the service manager with the problem. He concluded that they felt that they were dealing with an eighteen year old kid, and they were just going to wear him out. They did not even try to resolve the problem.

During that visit, Ron demanded that they give him a loaner car and he would keep it until they resolved the problem. He was told quite emphatically that he would not be getting a loaner car."

"I know they never want to do that," commented Dr. Howard.

"Then Ron walked back to me and told me to watch what happens next," said TJ. "I had no idea what to expect. Ron walked into the showroom where a salesman was in one of those small glassed-in sales offices, trying to close a deal with a prospective buyer. As he walked in, Ron told the prospective buyer that he could definitely expect to purchase a new vehicle. However, he should be informed that he will not get the complete service needed for his vehicle. He told the prospect that he has been suffering those consequences as a customer."

"I have never heard of anything like that being done before," expressed Dr. Howard.

"Ron didn't stop there," TJ went on. "He followed the same routine into the next sales cubicle where a sale was close to being consummated. Before he had a chance to enter a third cubicle, the sales manager presented himself and said, 'Let me talk to you for a minute.' A discussion ensued between Ron and the sales manager. He covered the circumstances and his dissatisfaction with the lack of effort to solve the problem of the rattle. Shortly thereafter, Ron was given a loaner."

"Really?" asked an intrigued Dr. Howard.

"Yes. Ron and I drove the loaner back to the campus," said TJ. "A few days later Ron got a call from the dealership, telling him that his car was ready to be picked up. The two of us drove the loaner car back to the dealership. I waited in the loaner car while Ron went for a test drive in his own car. By some miracle, the rattle was gone. Then Ron returned the loaner car to their parking lot. His final act was returning the keys to the service advisor that initially told him that he would never get a loaner car."

"That is really something," said Dr. Howard. "How many people would have taken that action? And at eighteen years old?"

"Ron explained to me later that you have to fight for everything," TJ said. How you fight depends on what arena you are in."

"I am understanding your admiration for your friend, Ron Mason," said Dr. Howard. "Let's get together next week. Would the same time be okay for you?"

"Yes, that would work," TJ confirmed.

TJ then left the office and headed back to the farm.

As scheduled, TJ was back to see Dr. Howard for his appointment a week later. After some small talk about working and activities since the last visit, Dr. Howard remarked at how impressed he was by hearing how Ron had solved the problem with the rattle in the car.

"I can understand why you were inspired by your friend and how much he meant to you," explained Dr. Howard. "I especially liked the part where he returned the keys to the service manager who told him that he would never get a loaner car."

"Yes, he had quite a sense of humor," commented TJ.

"Tell me something about his sense of humor," Dr. Howard requested, trying to get TJ to talk more about his good friend.

"There was one time when we were on leave. We weren't in uniform and we stopped at a local bar in town. While we were at the bar having a beer, this guy walked up to the bar next to Ron and ordered a beer. That patron was alone, drinking his beer while standing. It looked like he stopped for one beer and was then going to leave."

"Sounds like a quick stop before heading to his destination," commented Dr. Howard.

"I think so. While he was drinking his beer, Ron turned and said, 'How are you doing. Haven't seen you in a while.' The guy then asked if they knew each other. Then Ron said, 'You're used to seeing me in the monkey suit. I know I look different when I'm dressed in casual clothes.'

The guy then said, 'You might be confusing me with my brother.'

'No, just as I thought. It's hard to recognize me when I am dressed differently.' explained Ron."

"Then what happened?" asked Dr. Howard, following along.

"Shortly after that, the guy finished his beer. He told Ron that it was nice talking to him, but said that he had to get going.

'Nice seeing you again,' Ron responded.

Then the guy left. I asked Ron, 'Where do you know him from?'

Ron looked at me and responded, 'I never saw him before in my life!'

That was Ron. He could be a complete cut-up."

"That's funny," Dr. Howard commented. "Was Ron originally from Kansas?"

"No. We were both from Illinois," said TJ.

"Then how did Kansas get into the picture?" asked Dr. Howard.

"Ron vacationed with his parents during the time that we were in high school. He loved California. After that vacation, he and I talked often about going to California together. He talked so much about the mountains, deserts and the ocean. It was a definite plan of ours to go to California together. After I came back, I decided to fulfill the dream we had and go to California," TJ explained. "Even if I went myself."

"California is a unique place," said Dr. Howard. "I was there a few years ago for a convention. I can remember one morning looking into the parking lot of a restaurant. Two cars were parked next to each other. One had snow skis in a rack on the roof. The second car had a surfboard on his roof rack. I looked at those two cars and I was thinking that they represented two different seasons. Then it was explained to me that they would leave and go in different directions, but they would both be active in their desired sport at the same time that day. I know at that time I was thinking—California, what a great place to live."

"Yes, that's my destination," said TJ.

"But you're living in Kansas," clarified Dr. Howard.

"Only temporarily," explained TJ. I stopped to see one of our Marine buddies. He was injured and I stayed on to help his father at the farm."

"I see," said Dr. Howard.

"But I'm still planning to get to California."

"I will be going on vacation for about three weeks," said Dr. Howard. "We should plan to get together after that. Call my office in about three weeks and set up another appointment," explained Dr. Howard. "I did want to mention to you that I enjoy your stories about your friend, Ron. When you tell these stories, then he is still with us. It's an honor to him. I should mention something else that I think is very important. You haven't referred to him as your late friend. That's good. These stories continue to inform and entertain people."

"I never thought about it that way," said TJ.

"His legacy continues," said Dr. Howard.
"Thank you Dr. Howard. Have a good vacation."
"Thank you, TJ. See you later."

Chapter Fourteen

Tom's Dilemma

One night Tom said he had something important to discuss with TJ. When TJ asked Tom what it was about, Tom suggested that they take a ride and discuss it. The two of them got into TJ's truck and drove away. Butch rode along, as he had been accustomed to doing almost every evening. However, this time he sat in the back seat of TJ's truck.

TJ had no idea as to what Tom wanted to discuss with him. He started thinking about the last time that Tom wanted to talk to him privately like this. It was about the school presentation to discuss their time in combat in Afghanistan. Thinking about it, that led to him meeting Sandy. And that turned out to be a good result for TJ.

Rather than go to a bar or a coffee shop, Tom suggested that they go over to a park area a few miles away from the farm. He said that it would give them the privacy that they needed. After driving to what appeared to be a secluded area in the park, they got out. It was also an opportunity for TJ to give Butch a chance to walk around.

Tom started to tell TJ that the farm had been in the family for generations. It was the livelihood for his parents and his grandparents before then. TJ just looked at Tom and nodded, because he knew all that.

Tom then told him that his Dad had run into some financial problems relating to the farm before Tom came back from

Afghanistan. Being late on prior loans, Tom's Dad had been unable to get a loan from any of the banks.

He explained that his Dad responded to an advertisement from a place identified as The Loan Store (TLS). The loans were not traditional. In fact he didn't know if they were even legal. The interest rate was outrageous, but his Dad did not feel that he had much of a choice. Repayments were to be made in person in cash on a weekly basis.

After Tom was back working on the farm, his Dad explained the problem to him since he was having difficulty making the payments. That's when Tom found out that his Dad had secured the loan with the title to the farm. At that time, Tom decided to go with his Dad to meet with the people at TLS.

The location of the office was what someone could likely call a ghost town. It was an old strip mall where locations of small business units had once existed. It did not appear that any of the other units were currently occupied. Realistically, it looked like something that was ready to face demolition. The unit where they stopped at had a small sign indicating TLS next to the entrance to the door. The two of them met with an individual named Jack.

After discussing the problem with Jack, it was suggested that a new agreement be prepared. The result was higher payments and a higher interest rate. As much as they hated that turn of events, they both felt that they had no choice. His Dad had to avoid the payment that was presently due.

Payments were made for the next few months before payment problems surfaced again. Tom persuaded his Dad that he would go in and talk to Jack at TLS himself.

Tom explained to TJ that he drove to TLS himself and met with Jack. Before long Jack made him an offer. He would modify the payments if Tom could work for him. Jack explained that several people were behind with their payments. Jack needed Tom to make personal visits to customers with delinquent accounts. When Tom told Jack that he worked at the farm during the day,

Jack told him that it was better to make the personal contacts at night. This arrangement was not explained to Tom's Dad. Instead, Tom told his Dad that Jack was understanding of the problem.

Under the circumstances, Tom was feeling that he had no choice at that time. It became obvious to Tom that Jack was convinced that if he sent a former Marine out to do his collections, it would be very intimidating to the people behind on their loans. After two weeks, Tom realized that he could no longer be a collector for Jack and TLS under those circumstances.

When Tom tried to explain that to Jack, it did not go over well with Jack. He became very angry. However, Jack then told Tom that he was a very understanding person. He said he had another opportunity for Tom. This is where Tom said he was going to have difficulty explaining the new arrangement to TJ.

"I'll just come right out and tell you," Tom began. "The new deal was for me to distribute drugs."

"Really?" responded TJ. "And you agreed to do that?"

"Yes," answered Tom. "I rationalized. I was looking at recreational drug usage as a victimless act. And again, what choice did I have at that time, considering the situation with the farm?"

"I know you're not doing that now because I'm with you most of the time," responded TJ.

"No. You're right. As you can understand, that arrangement changed when I got injured at the farm," explained Tom.

"What about the loan?" asked TJ

"My Dad has been able to keep up with most of it."

"That's good," said TJ.

"Well, here's where things get crazy," Tom went on.

"Crazier?" commented TJ

"Yes. You see my Dad had a visit from an oil company rep some time ago. He wanted to discuss an offer for my Dad. Apparently, they think there is oil under the farm property," explained Tom.

"Really?" commented a surprised TJ.

"Yes. Oil in Kansas. Unreal. Then, of course, the farm is not that far from Oklahoma," said Tom. "They offered to give Dad a sizable upfront amount before they started drilling. And what's great is that they would be doing it on only part of the farm. Dad could continue to do his farming."

"That sounds great," assured TJ

"With the money, Dad would be able to pay off the loan to TLS."

"Problem solved," said TJ.

"No it's not," countered Tom.

"Why not?" asked TJ.

"You see, I went to TLS and told Jack that the loan would be paid off," said Tom. "And then Jack asked me how that could be done. That's when I opened my big fuckin mouth and told him about the oil deal. Sometime I can't believe that I have such a big mouth."

"Well so what," said TJ. "What difference does it make where the money comes from?"

"Because that's when Jack told me to read the fine print in Dad's loan agreement," Tom explained. "He told me that he was a partner with my Dad. Then he tried to assure me that my Dad would still be in good shape."

"What do you want to do?" asked TJ.

"I'm no lawyer, but, when he wasn't there, I looked at the paperwork my Dad had and I think Jack is giving me a line of bullshit," explained Tom. "I need to go see Jack. But I would feel more comfortable if you were with me."

"Okay. We'll go together," TJ agreed. "When do you want to go?"

"Tomorrow. The sooner, the better."

The next day came fast enough. Tom and TJ finished their farm chores for the day. Tom told his Dad that he and TJ were going to take a ride into town that night. Shortly after dinner, the two of them left in TJ's truck. As was the routine with TJ, Butch rode in the back seat of the truck.

As they arrived at the old strip mall, TJ could see, as Tom had described, it was a set of rundown single story buildings. It did not appear to have any tenants, except for the one location with the initials TLS next to the door. It was easy to see why it was described as a ghost town. It was probably going to be torn down in the near future, if and when, somebody bought the property to build on it.

TJ parked across from the location. He and Tom got out of the truck and walked toward the building. Butch remained in the back seat of the truck. Tom knocked on the door. They could see that someone looked out of the peephole. The door was then opened by Jack's assistant, Ray.

"Come in," said Jack. "Have a seat," as he cautiously eyed TJ.

"This is my friend, TJ," Tom opened. "He and I served in the Marines together."

"Okay," responded Jack. "What can I do for you?"

"Well," Tom hesitated, "I need to talk about the situation concerning my Dad's farm and the discussion we were having."

"Tom, is your friend an attorney?" Jack questioned.

"No. He's just a good friend of mine," responded Tom.

"Then I can only discuss the matter with you, Tom," said Jack. "This is a private business matter."

"But I asked him to be here with me," Tom went on.

"No," Jack abruptly answered. "It does not concern him. Mr. Marine, do us a favor and wait outside until we're done in here discussing our business."

TJ looked at Tom and nodded. Then he got up, walked to the door, and left. As TJ walked out, he glanced back at Ray, who stood in the back of the office during the abbreviated conversation. After the door was closed by Ray, TJ walked back to the truck and got in to wait for Tom.

About fifteen minutes later, Tom walked out of the office and the door was closed behind him. He got into the truck and said, "Let's go."

TJ started the truck and drove off. Nothing was said for several minutes as they drove away.

Then Tom said, "Those guys really piss me off."

"What happened?" questioned TJ.

"They're dead set on going into a partnership with my Dad for the farm'" explained Tom. "Jack kept saying that it was in the contract."

"But you looked at the contract," countered TJ. "That's just not true. Your father is not bound by anything."

"I know," answered Tom. "Then they brought up the drugs."

"What do you mean?"

"He said they have pictures of me with the drugs," answered Tom. "Their story is that I worked for them as a collector. However, they claim that they found out that I was also dealing in drugs. They assured me that they have some of the people that I collected from who will testify that I tried to sell them drugs. When Jack found out that I was a drug dealer, they terminated me."

"That's their story?" asked TJ.

"Yes. Those fuckin bastards. That would destroy my family," reasoned Tom.

"What are you going to do?" asked TJ.

"I don't know. I have to think about it," said Tom.

Very few words were spoken during the rest of the drive to the farm.

✦

Chapter Fifteen

Tom's Solution

The next day at the farm was as typical of any other day. Then Tom told TJ that the following day at the farm would be a short one. Tom would be taking his father for his annual physical, which included several tests that would be administered to his father. The appointment was set for as late as possible in the afternoon. Tom's Dad always set them that way in order not to interfere with his farm activities.

When they had a moment together, Tom told TJ that he decided what he would do regarding the TLS group. He said that he had to go over there to get things straightened out once and for all. Whatever the consequences were, he had to get things resolved.

TJ looked directly at Tom and said, "You can't go."

"What do you mean?" responded Tom. "I have to go. I can't let them confront my Dad. There's no stopping them."

"You know how valuable you are to the farm and your family," reasoned TJ. "That kind of confrontation will put you in harm's way."

"I have no choice. That's what we were trained to do, right? I can't turn my back on a situation that might be difficult. These guys need to know that I won't back down."

"I'm just looking at the whole picture, for you and for your family," said TJ.

"I am too," responded Tom. "If they follow through and I end up in prison as a drug dealer, so be it. I just can't sell my Dad down the river for these bastards."

TJ knew Tom well enough to see that, realistically, no matter how hard he tried, he was not going to persuade him to change his plans.

"Okay, you're right I understand what you're saying," said TJ, appearing to follow along and agree with Tom. "When do you plan to go?"

"Tomorrow. I need to take my Dad to the clinic tomorrow for an exam and to have them administer some tests done," explained Tom. "His doctor said it shouldn't be delayed any longer."

As planned, the next work day was a short one. Tom left with his Dad and drove to the clinic for the anticipated exam and tests. They left just after four o'clock in the afternoon. The trip would take an hour, which was time enough for the scheduled appointment at five thirty. They expected to be back at a reasonable time for a late dinner.

After they left, TJ informed Tom's mother that he would be taking a ride into town. When she asked if he would be gone for a while, he told her that he would not be coming back late. In fact, he said he probably might be back before Tom and his Dad returned.

TJ and Butch got into the pick-up truck and left. About a couple of miles down the road, TJ pulled over to the side of the road and turned off the engine. He unlocked the glove compartment and took out his pistol. After loading the pistol, he reached under the seat and pulled out a holster. It was the special holster. After lifting his right loose fitting pants leg, he secured the holster to the calf of his right leg and then pulled down the loose fitting leg of his jeans.

He started the truck and drove away, heading toward town. Twenty minutes later, he arrived at the industrial area where TLS was located. It was after the usual working hours and there was little traffic on the roads in the area. He drove to the location of TLS and parked the truck. Before getting out, he made sure the windows were opened to give Butch the air he needed. He then got out of the truck and walked toward the entrance of TLS.

TJ knocked on the door. He noticed that the peep hole was being used as he waited. A surprised Jack opened the door and TJ walked in.

Jack then walked back to his desk and sat down. He looked back at TJ and said, "Can I help you?"

"Maybe."

Jack looked at him and then said, "Wait. You're Tom's buddy. Now I remember. What can I help you with? Were you looking for a job?"

TJ sat down in the chair in from of the desk where Jack was sitting. He looked at Jack and said, "I'm aware that you helped Tom's dad."

"That's right. We're in the business of helping people," responded Jack. "What's this all about?"

"Well, in helping his Dad, you made a lot of money. But he won't be needing your help anymore," TJ explained.

"That's none of your business. Who the hell do you think you're talking to?" Jack retorted in an angry tone. "I would advise you to get the hell out of here and don't think about coming back."

"Your business with that family is over," TJ stated, looking directly at Jack as he remained seated.

Just then, Jack's assistant, Ray, came through a doorway from the back room behind TJ. He was holding a pistol and pointing it at TJ. Ray then walked over and locked the front door.

"You're dealing with the wrong people, soldier boy," Jack told TJ. "I can see you're not going to leave quietly."

TJ just stared back at Jack.

"No punk soldier boy is going to come in here and mess up my operation. It's a shame that you couldn't find work. So you decided to rob our business. During your failed robbery attempt, you were shot and killed by the owner. That's how the report is going to read."

Just then, something suddenly slammed against the front door, creating a loud sound, and getting the attention of the three of them.

Jack looked at Ray. "Are you expecting anyone?"

"No," responded Ray, looking at the door.

"Every once in a while, some homeless bum tries to see if one of these businesses is occupied so they can spend the night. Check it out," Jack directed Ray.

Ray walked over to the door, gun in hand, and unlocked the door. As he opened the door, he looked outside. Not seeing anybody, he looked back at Jack and said, "Nothing."

Just then, Butch appeared out of nowhere and lunged at Ray, causing him to fall backwards, dropping his gun to the floor. Ray immediately reached for the gun.

With a trained military response, TJ pulled up his right pants leg, pulled out his pistol and shot Ray twice in the torso as Ray was aiming his gun at Butch. During that momentary confrontation, Jack opened his top desk drawer and pulled out a pistol. As Jack was raising his gun to fire, TJ turned and fired two shots into Jack's chest, causing him to fall backwards against his chair and roll to the floor.

All the activity took place within seconds. TJ checked each of the men as they lay there with their guns in their hands. Both were dead. It was over. TJ holstered his pistol. He then walked over to the door. He walked out of the building with Butch, closing the door behind them.

As he looked around, TJ saw nobody in that industrial area. He opened the truck door and let Butch in. He then drove away. After TJ was within a couple of miles from the farm, he pulled over and stopped at the side of the road. He let Butch out for a moment and then placed a call to Tom on his cell phone. Tom answered.

"It's TJ. Where are you now?" he asked.

"We're on our way back. Maybe twenty minutes from the farm," Tom responded.

"After you get your Dad home, meet me at the park where we stopped before," TJ instructed.

"Okay, what's up?"

"I'll let you know as soon as you get here."

Tom arrived about forty minutes later.

"What's going on?" Tom asked as he jumped out of his truck.

"Don't go over to TLS, not now or ever again," TJ told Tom.

"Why? What happened?" questioned Tom.

"You know, those two bastards that pissed you off."

"Yes."

"Well, they will piss no more."

"What?" questioned Tom.

"I know you felt that you had an obligation to take care of things. As you reminded me, that's how we were trained," explained TJ. "But I had an obligation myself. I could not let one of my buddies leave his family after coming home safely from Afghanistan."

"But what happened?" pursued Tom.

"I tried to reason with them about the situation. Unfortunately, they were not the type to reason with," explained TJ. "They're gone from the scene. No forwarding address. The matter is resolved. End of story."

"Now what?" asked Tom.

"Well, I will be leaving. It's time I made my way to California. I never intended to be in Kansas this long," reasoned TJ. "You need to be here for your family and for the farm. As far as your perspective, any matters with TLS never happened."

TJ and Tom drove back to the farm that night in their trucks. Butch was sitting in the front seat of TJ's truck, just looking forward at the road. TJ looked over at Butch.

"I wish I knew more about your background. I heard that your old master was a veteran. But sometimes I wonder if you were a member of the military yourself. Part of the canine corp? I guess I'll never know. Either way, you saved my life."

TJ reached over, put his hand on Butch's head and then his back and gently stroked his fur. Butch just looked back at TJ. TJ would swear that when Butch looked back at him, he had a smile on his face.

Chapter Sixteen

On the Road

The next morning TJ gathered his belongings and said good bye to Tom and Tom's family. Then he and Butch left. There was one more stop he had to make. Sandy had completed her teaching for the year. She was probably spending her time at home just reading from her assortment of books while she collected her unemployment benefits.

It was somewhat of a surprise to have TJ stop by her apartment, especially during the late morning hour. Usually, they met in the evenings.

"Well, hello stranger," she greeted him. "What brings you here at this hour?"

"I'm moving on," he answered. "I realized that farming wasn't for me."

"What do you mean, moving on?" she responded. "Are you trying to say good bye?"

"You knew about my California plans," TJ said. "This shouldn't be a surprise to you."

"It is a surprise to me. I know about California, but the timing is throwing me off," she reasoned.

"I don't know what else to say," said TJ.

"Well I do. Take me with you."

"You can't mean that," responded a surprised TJ. "You have your entire career here. You're a teacher. I'm sure you don't want to walk away from that."

"Don't forget, I was given a pink slip," she tried to explain. "I've given my all to my career. They were good years. I enjoyed them. But then I found something that made a difference for me. I fell in love. I don't want to lose you. I feel very special when I'm with you."

"And you are very special to me. I've never met anyone in my life like you. This is very difficult for me too. But I can't stay here. I need to go," he said.

"Okay. I mean it. Take me with you," she said.

"You would really do that, considering what you might be giving up?" he asked.

"I'm looking at what I'm gaining, not what I'm giving up. We can't predict what will happen next. If necessary, we can fish from the pier. We'll eat what we catch. Maybe we'll both get part time jobs. Together we can make a life that we can't even see at this time. But we can do it together, creating memories."

During the rest of the day, Sandy made arrangement to give up her leased vehicle and her apartment. Later that evening, they left in TJ's truck as a full moon lit up the night sky. From the rear of the truck, one could see the silhouette of two people in the truck heading west. Then, occasionally one would be able to see the silhouette of a third companion that would appear from the back seat of the vehicle.

As is known to all, life can take twists and turns and lead one in different directions with various results. Where this venture would go, no one can say for sure. But the three of them were looking forward to life's next chapter.

After graduating from Northwestern University School of Business, Frederick Bruce became a business counselor to small businesses. Clients ranged in size from one to ten people. Bruce later pursued a law career. He is currently a practicing attorney.

Although engaged in his law practice, Bruce has studied history and followed current events. In this, his fourth novel, he portrays the post military life of a combat veteran and the mindset that exists when assimilating back into a civilian culture. Although not a complete analysis of the paths of all veterans, it expresses the experiences of one veteran to which many can identify.

The second and third books written by Frederick Bruce were murder mysteries— Murder at the Cathedral and Sex, Murder, Betrayal. His first book, The Blue Car, A Trilogy, tells the stories of three individuals seeking perfect lifetime careers. The stories were characterized by BlueInk Review as being told with a "pay it forward" symbolism.

Over the years, Bruce has worked with, and found the lives of people and their related stories very interesting. Although fictional, his experience has enabled him to share many stories about people based on real events.